Praise for BERNARD PEPPERLIN:

A *Kirkus Reviews* Best Book of the Year!

"Hoffman deftly creates a compellingly different kind of Wonderland, a place with its own set of realities and whose residents understand that, in spite of their differences, they are stronger together than apart. Everything a fantasy should be and more."

—*Kirkus Reviews* (starred review)

"A quirky flight of fancy with a rich lineage."

—*Publishers Weekly*

"Hoffman cleverly mingles familiar themes and tropes from Carroll's famous novel with wry humor. A great read-alike for fans of Roald Dahl, E. B. White, and Katherine Applegate."

—*School Library Journal*

"Bernard and his newfound friends—revolutionary rats, wise-cracking cats, and coffee-chugging squirrels, to name a few—will delight and inspire readers of all ages. New York City will never be the same again!"

—Erin Entrada Kelly, Newbery Medal–winning author
of *Hello, Universe*

BERNARD
PEPPERLIN

CARA HOFFMAN

HARPER
An Imprint of HarperCollinsPublishers

ISBN 978-0-06-286544-1 (trade bdg.) — ISBN 978-0-06-286545-8 (pbk.)

Typography by Laura Mock
20 21 22 23 24 PC/LSCH 10 9 8 7 6 5 4 3
❖

For E and Em

♣ ♥ 1 ♦ ♠

A Swim in the Drink

The Dormouse had been trying hard to stay awake. First he ate a sugar cube. Then he pinched himself. Then he tried climbing on top of the rickety table instead of sitting in his chair. The table was set for a tea party and the cups and plates clattered as he moved past them. Crusts of toast were scattered over the white cloth and in the center stood a blue china teapot decorated with a picture of three bridges and a winding river that let out into the sea.

He stood on a package of biscuits to look around but couldn't see her anymore. The curious girl with the long blond hair must have left the party when he'd nodded off. Daytime was hard if you were nocturnal. Especially if it never ended.

"He's sleepwalking again," said the March Hare.

"Well, get him *down*," said the Hatter. "Before he steps in the butter."

"I'm awake," said the Dormouse.

"You always say that," said the March Hare. "And it's rarely true."

The Hatter poured a drop of tea onto the Dormouse's nose and it burned like a little spark. He yelped, his whiskers stiffening, tears forming in the corners of his eyes.

The Dormouse wished he had gone with the girl. She was wearing a blue dress and a white apron, and floating beside her was a large cat. The cat had an elegant striped coat and was grinning from ear to ear, its teeth gleaming in the late-afternoon sun. Or at least that's what he thought he had seen. There was no sight of them now, and cats rarely floated, so it might have been a dream.

But dream or not, the Dormouse wanted to run after them. He wanted to walk out of the garden and down the lane, but he knew he couldn't make it past the front gate. None of them could.

Because for the Dormouse and the March Hare and the Mad Hatter, time had stopped. They couldn't walk along a new path or meet a new person or go to a new place.

The day that time stopped had started out fine. The Hatter was to sing at a party. But his song was so terrible, so loud and boring and long, that Time itself became furious and walked out on them. Forcing them to live forever at half past teatime on Sunday afternoon.

It wasn't so bad in the beginning. It was exciting, even.

Because of the Hatter's song, the sun was always golden, the roses never died, and the brambles never needed pruning. There were always scones to eat and buttered toast, delicious black tea with cream. And none of them—not the Dormouse, nor the March Hare, nor the Mad Hatter—had grown a day older or an inch fatter since four o'clock, August 14, 1889.

But very soon things changed. Few creatures ventured out to the garden to visit them at their long table, and without time, dreaming was the only way to leave the garden, or have visitors, or do anything new.

Worst of all was being with the Mad Hatter. He bragged and stood on his chair in muddy boots. He spoke with his mouth full and guzzled all the tea. And there was no way to avoid him, sitting there at the same table in the same garden on the same day that could never, ever end.

The Dormouse stood on his toes so he could see

out through the gate, but all he could see were the tips of the cat's ears and the girl's pale hair shining in the sunlight as she walked away. Then a moment later she took a sip from a tiny bottle and disappeared entirely.

"Why did she leave?" the Dormouse asked.

"Well, she was no good at riddles, so she decided to go," said the March Hare.

"And songs," said the Hatter. "She was no good at songs."

The Hatter's skin was a ruddy pink and his pale eyes bulged slightly beneath unruly gray eyebrows. He wore a top hat on his large head, which seemed enormous compared to his skinny body, and he was dressed as though he had just come from performing at a concert. He reached across the table for a slice of bread, used it to wipe a smear of raspberry jam off his face, then ate it.

"You of all people should not talk about *songs*," said the March Hare gravely.

The March Hare was bucktoothed and easily startled. He spoke quickly, like most hares do, and he was used to making the best of a bad situation. He poured himself another cup of tea, spooning in four heaps of sugar and stirring vigorously.

The Dormouse gazed out at the winding cobbled paths beyond the trees and flower beds. *If only I could be alone*, he thought, *and take that path. If only night could come and I could see stars in the sky, watch the sunrise, and hear morning birds singing. If only I could swim in a river or hear a clock tick, or meet new people, or talk to other mice.*

"I wish she would come back," the Dormouse said, thinking he should have tucked himself into the girl's pocket.

The Mad Hatter ignored him. He was busy prying his watch apart with a butter knife and slathering butter on the gears. The March Hare sipped his tea. His hands trembled as he set the cup down, and it clattered against the saucer.

"How much tea have you had?" the Dormouse asked his friend drowsily.

"Since time stopped?" said the March Hare. "Fifty-six thousand, five hundred and seventy-five cups. Why do you ask?"

The smell of roses and warm tea and milk made the Dormouse's head nod forward.

"He's falling asleep again!" said the Hatter, pulling a pin from his hat to poke the Dormouse.

"He can't help it," said the March Hare. "The *dor* in *dormouse* comes from the French word *dormir*, which means 'to sleep.'"

The Hatter stuck the March Hare with the pin instead.

The Dormouse heard his friend yelp but he could barely keep his eyes open. His head nodded forward and he sank into a little pool of honey that had gathered at the edge of his saucer.

"He needs more tea!" said the Hatter, yanking the Dormouse toward the great blue teapot.

Jerking awake and startled by the commotion, the Dormouse grabbed at whatever was in reach—watch gears, sugar bowls, the edge of the tablecloth. He knocked plates and cups and silverware to the ground.

"Let him go!" cried the March Hare, grasping the Dormouse's tail and trying to pull him away from the Hatter. The Dormouse kicked at each of them in turn, fighting with all his might to get free. At last, the Hatter grabbed the Dormouse around the waist. He lifted him high off the table and plunged him, snout first, into the scalding darkness of the steaming blue teapot.

And then something truly remarkable happened.

Instead of fighting and thrashing and squirming his way out of the teapot—as he had done before—the Dormouse shut his eyes, pushed his head farther in, and began to swim with all his might. He swam away from the Mad Hatter and the March Hare, away from the garden, away from the table and the never-ending tea party. He plunged down and down, unable to feel the bottom of the teapot beneath his paws. Someone was still yanking his tail, but he swam harder, until they lost their grip. He swam down, down, down, holding his breath. Soon the tea was no longer hot but cold as ice, and his heart was beating fast in his chest.

He opened his eyes and a vast murky world swirled before him, green and cut through with rippling bands of light. A fish as large as the March Hare swam past, its scaly tail sliding along his side. He kicked, not knowing which way was up or down, pulled by the current and tumbling in the water until he broke through the shining surface, coughing and gasping and miraculously free.

♣ ♥ 2 ♦ ♠

Advice from a Cat

The Dormouse stared up at the world around him, shivering and sputtering as he thrashed in the cold water.

At first, he thought he must be in the middle of the ocean. But no, he could see coastline on either side. He bobbed along on a current, stunned by the new world. A bright sun shone down upon him and the air was crisp.

This must be a dream, he thought. Above him a vast steel-cabled bridge stretched from one shore to the other. Strange houses lined either side of the shore, enormous and square, rising into the air as tall as a forest. Some looked like they were made entirely from windows, which twinkled orange in the early-morning light.

He had never in his life had a dream this real. Suddenly he was startled by the deafening blast of a horn and spun around in the water, wide-eyed as a great ship sped past. Dozens of people stood on the deck of the ship, their hair blowing in the breeze as they gazed out over the dark green water.

The horn's blast seemed to open his ears and eyes and nose all at once. He no longer smelled roses and tea but the sharp, salty scent of brackish river water and a touch of factory smoke. Voices of large white birds called to one another as they glided on currents of air above his head. If this was a river, he thought, it had to be the biggest river any mouse had ever known.

The sky above him was a gleaming blue. The river waved and rippled, catching the sun, which shone like silver coins cast out on the water.

The Dormouse had never felt so awake in his life! So much to see and hear and smell and taste. He paddled quickly with all his paws. Now he could see there was not just one bridge stretching from shore to shore but three! A long silver train clattered over one of the bridges and there were tiny figures walking and running and riding bicycles over it too. But strangest of all were the square boats with wheels that traveled over the land faster than anything he had ever seen. He thought again that he must be dreaming and pinched himself quite hard to make sure he was awake.

And then he saw it!

On the far bank of the river, a tall brick building with the word *Watchtower* glowing on its surface beamed out over the river. Above the word *Watchtower* was an enormous round clock. The hands on the clock pointed to the two and the eight. It was ten past eight! The Dormouse caught his breath and then let out a tremendous whoop of joy, slapping at the water around him. He spun in a circle, laughing in delight. He felt like he could soar. It was ten past eight in the *morning*! And he was alone at last, just as he had wished. He was alone and he was swimming and nothing was the same! He had found the place where time had gone!

The Dormouse began to swim quickly toward the clock and the town of towering houses, but just then another ship whizzed past, sending him bobbing and sailing on a wave to the other shore. He landed with a thunk on the weedy riverbank, soaked to the skin but happy.

The shore was covered with bottles and bags and long strange pins, driftwood and glass and fishing line. The Dormouse found a patch of soft sand and lay on his back, still reeling from the new sights and smells, staring up into the blue sky, where birds circled and swooped. He watched them fly over the bustling bridges, and then up and up and up, above the glimmering forest of buildings that seemed to stretch on forever. At last. He was safe from the Hatter.

This was indeed, he thought, a magnificent new world.

Just as he was beginning to drift off into a reverie, he heard a low, gravelly voice.

"Hey, pal," it said. "This ain't exactly the best place to take a nap."

The voice came from a grizzled-looking animal with black-and-white fur, who was staring down at him. The animal had long, drooping whiskers and gleaming yellow eyes. He was holding a small fishing pole and chewed on a thin sliver of white bone, narrow as a toothpick. The animal grinned and the tip of its tail twitched. Suddenly the Dormouse realized it was a cat, a lean, battle-scarred cat. The cat winked and a cold shiver went up the Dormouse's spine.

There was a bucket of small freshly caught fish near its feet. *Good,* the Dormouse thought, *this cat musn't be hungry for mice. At least not right now.*

The Dormouse hopped to his feet and looked the cat in the eye. Speaking in a clear and friendly voice, he said, "I beg your pardon, sir. I'm new here."

"That," said the cat, smiling wryly, "I gathered." It was then the Dormouse noticed that one of the cat's ears was smaller than the other, as though it had been snipped with scissors. It looked like it must have been painful. *This cat has had his own troubles in the past,* the Dormouse thought. And something about that made the cat seem familiar, like they could be friends.

"You got a name?" the cat asked.

The Dormouse's heart swelled, and he thought he

might laugh for no reason at all. No one had ever asked him his name before. Not the Hatter, not the March Hare, no one.

"Yes, I do!" he said, raising himself up to his full height and reaching out to shake hands. "My name is Bernard. Bernard Pepperlin. And I'm very pleased to meet you."

♣ ♥ **3** ♦ ♠

A Forest of Glimmering Buildings

"Pleased to meet *you*, Bernard," the cat said, taking the thin white bone from his mouth and showing a row of sharp white teeth. His eyes shone bright in the sun. "My name is Mittens."

"Mittens," the Dormouse said.

"There an echo in here? Yeah. Mittens. You got a problem with that?"

"Oh, no, Mittens is a lovely name," Bernard said.

"It'll do," the cat said. "You'd be surprised how many people got an opinion about it."

A breeze blew in off the river and Bernard could feel his fur drying beneath the warm sun. In the distance he heard a sound like a whistle, and somewhere geese were honking. The cat stretched and stuck the bone toothpick back in his mouth. Then he folded up his fishing poles and hid them beneath some jagged rocks at the edge of the beach. Bernard half expected the cat would fade into the air around them and disappear altogether, leaving just his smile behind. Such things were not uncommon back in the garden. But the cat stayed right where he was, regarding Bernard with a look of concern.

"So, lissen, like I was saying," said the cat. "You gotta be *care*ful around here. Civilized people like you and me might sleep when the sun comes up. But you gotta understand. This ain't the place for it. Know what I mean?"

"I'm afraid I don't," said Bernard.

"I *mean*," said Mittens, "you sleep here and the Pork Pie Gang is gonna get you."

"I see," said Bernard. But he didn't really understand what Mittens was talking about at all. He looked out again at the clock, which now read eight thirty, and smiled. He wasn't particularly afraid of people who ate pork pies. And it was hard to believe they could be worse than the Hatter. Though he knew pork pie was also the name of a hat, so maybe they were related somehow.

"What do they look like?" Bernard asked.

"Oh, you'd know them if you see them!" said Mittens. "They kinda slouch like this." He sank into his hips and pushed out his belly. "And their fur is like *this*." He shook himself out until his fur looked puffy and shaggy. "And their teeth are like *this*." He stuck out his lower jaw and flared his nostrils. "And their breath smells like pickles."

None of that sounded the least bit dangerous to Bernard. "Thanks for the warning," he said politely.

"Oh, *and*," Mittens said, "they carry spears and clubs and knives and ukuleles."

"Oh!" Bernard said, the hair on the back of his neck standing up. He didn't know what a ukulele was but it sounded terrifying.

"Quit shaking," Mittens said. "You'll be fine. But you gotta watch out 'cause they're not real nice and they like to steal stuff."

"I don't have any stuff," Bernard said.

"Then they might steal *you*," Mittens said. "Lissen, it's been great meeting you, Bernard, but I gotta get to work." Then he picked up his bucket of fish and began walking gracefully up the embankment, avoiding the bottles, pins, chunks of wood, and bricks that lay strewn about.

"Wait," Bernard called as he scurried up the beach,

suddenly frightened. "Please! I don't know where I am. I have so many questions."

Mittens turned around and gazed at Bernard with his big yellow eyes. He said, "Do I look like Wikipedia to you?"

"Like a wika what? No. I . . . But—" Bernard shrugged. "I—"

The cat sighed. "All right," he said gruffly. "C'mon, then, hop up." Mittens leaned down so that Bernard could sit on his shoulder, and together they headed off, away from the speeding ships and rippling river, strolling beneath the shadow of the marvelous bridges, out into the vast wide world.

♣ ♥ 4 ♦ ♠

Dragon Fruit

The shiny boats with wheels whizzed by on the ground. Bernard had thought he heard geese honking but the noise was really coming from these boats.

"What *are* those?" Bernard asked.

"Buddy, you really ain't from around here, are you?" Mittens said. "Those are *cars*. The big ones are called trucks. The yellow ones are called taxicabs. You gotta watch out for them because they run you over."

Mittens slinked briskly along the riverbank, until they reached a wide wooden road where an enormous ship was docked and the fast cars and taxis pulled up to let people off. Gray birds walked among the people, pecking the ground and searching for crumbs. He could smell food cooking, something like meat or baking bread, strange smells he had never smelled before.

It seemed that suddenly the place was full of people rushing past. Men and women and children of all sizes and shapes and colors. Bernard had seen people and places like this only in books. He climbed on top of Mittens's head to get a better view. Suddenly he caught a glimpse of a girl with blond hair. She was walking fast beside her mother, wearing a blue dress.

"Look, there she is," he said. "I knew she must have been from a magical place."

"There who is?" Mittens asked.

But then the girl turned and he saw it wasn't her at all.

"No one," said Bernard forlornly. "Never mind. Why are they all rushing so fast?"

"This is New York," Mittens said. "People got places to be. Even I got places to be. I gotta get up to the Empire Diner before the lunch rush. But first I gotta go to my morning job."

"How many jobs do you have?"

"A bunch," said Mittens. "I wake up before the sun to go fishing, head over to my morning job at the diner, then spend the rest of the day working in a bodega."

"What's a bodega?"

"It's a human word that means 'warehouse.' But it ain't really a warehouse. It's more like a grocery store."

"What do you do there?"

"I make sure nobody's snacking on the merchandise."

"Why do you have so many jobs?"

"Like I told you, this is New York. You gotta hustle to stay ahead."

Mittens turned from the pier and walked across

a great road, then took a smaller side street directly into the majestic forest of buildings. The place smelled amazing: sooty like chimneys and sweet like pastry or pipe smoke, bitter like buried roots and fragrant like the scent of flowery tea. There were many shops with awnings and, beneath them, piles and piles of vegetables and fruit and strange-looking fish laid out upon beds of ice.

Mittens stopped in front of a fish market and set down his bucket, waiting until a fat orange cat with soulful blue eyes came out and nodded at them. The orange cat was wearing a stained rubber apron. He had a pencil tucked behind his ear and carried a tiny notebook. This cat was all business; he pulled some paper out of his apron pocket and handed it to Mittens, then picked up the bucket of fish and went back into the shop.

Trucks parked by the curb, the drivers unloading crates of oranges, bananas, and chestnuts. They unloaded ginger and long green beans and oddly shaped red fruits that Bernard had never seen before. As they walked along he saw buckets of eels and small blue crabs, and shops full of tiny pies, enormous cookies, and pastries as round as a rubber ball covered with sesame seeds. The smells of the strange, delicious food filled the air and suddenly Bernard was struck with a deep pain in his belly.

"I think I might be sick," he told Mittens. "My stomach feels strange."

The cat laughed. "I think you might be hungry," he said. "Don't worry, we'll be at the diner soon. They'll give us breakfast there."

At the word *breakfast*, Bernard wrapped his arms around himself. His stomach made a sound like a wild animal inside him needed to be fed. Somehow, he was happy to feel the strange ache again. *It's better to feel than not to feel*, he told himself.

They walked past a fruit stand and the cat's paw flashed out. In an instant he had swiped up a chunk of the strange red fruit they had seen earlier. Mittens handed it to Bernard. On the inside it was white and pulpy.

"This is dragon fruit," the cat said. "Eat up. It will tide you over."

Bernard crunched into the fruit. It was sweet and mild and juicy like a pear. He soon devoured it all and felt wide awake and even hungrier.

"What do you do at the diner?" Bernard asked.

"I work for the queen," said Mittens.

"There's a queen of New York?" Bernard said.

"Of course," Mittens said. "Say, where do you come from anyway?"

"It's a bit hard to explain," said Bernard.

"Try me," said Mittens.

Bernard told Mittens the story of the garden. He told him about the Hatter and the March Hare. He told him there was a queen where he came from too and that she was no one you would go to for help. She dressed all in red and was always calling for someone to be punished.

Mittens listened, his face growing serious and his tail twitching.

"That's some story," the cat said. "You're a brave mouse, Bernard."

"I try to be," said Bernard.

"This Hatter sounds like a real lunatic," said Mittens.

"He wasn't always," said Bernard. "He made hats for a living, using a powerful kind of glue that made you dizzy. He breathed in too many fumes from the glue, and it made him behave terribly."

"Yeah, well, glue or no glue—no one should be shoving you into a teapot. That just ain't right."

Atop Mittens's shoulder, Bernard marveled at the sights on the crowded narrow street. Soon the food markets gave way to shops filled with clothing, pots and pans, and toys, all in bright colors and patterns. But when they turned a corner he crouched lower on the cat's shoulder, trying to make himself invisible.

There, slouching against a crate full of green mechanical frogs, stood a scruffy, shaggy creature in a short-brimmed hat with a feather sticking out of its band. Bernard had seen drawings in books of people wearing such things. There was no mistaking it.

It was a pork pie hat.

The creature wearing it had narrow eyes and a smug expression on its face. He could see what Mittens meant. For one, Bernard couldn't tell exactly what sort of animal it was—it might have been a large rat or small stray dog, or even a weasel who had seen better days. At its feet was a black case that looked like it was made for a tiny guitar. Mittens hissed under his breath as they walked past, but the creature didn't seem scared at all.

"They think they run this city," Mittens told Bernard once they had walked farther down the street. "But don't let them fool you. The people who really run the city are underground."

When Mittens and Bernard reached the end of the block, the cat stopped in front of a small door. He knocked three times. After a long moment the door opened and an ancient rat poked her head out. Her eyes were shiny and alert, and her face was wrinkled. She sniffed at Bernard and smiled, showing her sharp gray teeth.

"Good morning, Mittens," she said. "I see you've caught yourself a nice little snack for later."

♣ ♥ 5 ♦ ♠

A Dance Underground

Bernard's blood went cold in his veins and he felt like he couldn't breathe. Then Mittens and the old rat began laughing, which made it even worse. Tears welled in Bernard's eyes, and he began trembling.

"Sophie!" Mittens said. "You know I ain't that kind of cat. I could never eat a mouse."

"Mittens the mouse hunter. The only bodega cat in the city who could never eat a mouse," she said. "But maybe someday."

"Maybe never," Mittens said. "Why do I gotta keep telling everybody I'm a pescatarian? Lissen, you want to eat mice, be my guest, but—"

At this Bernard let out a little shriek and Mittens put his paw on his small shoulder to comfort him. "Oh, sorry, Bernard. Not you, not you."

"No, he's right," Sophie said. "Not you. You've got a special spark. And any friend of Mittens is a friend of mine."

She stepped aside, letting them into a long dark passage that seemed to run beneath the building.

It was cool and damp inside the passage. At one point Bernard could see light coming in through a grate above their heads. The place smelled like cinders, and even though they were underground, he thought he heard the faint sound of a train whistle.

Sophie squinted at him. She sniffed him again and this time she said, "What brought you to the city?"

"I don't know exactly," said Bernard. "I think . . . I think I just couldn't sit any longer in the garden. There was no one like me to talk to. There was no time."

Sophie and Mittens exchanged a serious look.

"Whaddaya mean there was no time?" Mittens asked.

"There was no *time*," he said again. "The Hatter's song was so terrible it stopped time. It was the same day every day. No one different ever came to the garden. It was the same loud voices and the same stories and the same food. There was no one else for me to talk to."

"Have you told him?" Sophie asked Mittens.

"I ain't said a thing," Mittens said.

"Told me what?" Bernard asked.

"All in good time," Sophie said, a twinkle in her eye. "Come on, the queen will be waiting."

Mittens and Bernard followed the wise old rat through a narrow tunnel underground. It wound through several twists and turns like a maze and Bernard felt quite lost. Just when he was beginning to think it had no end, he saw a light in the distance and heard a booming voice say, "Stand clear of the closing doors, please." Then the narrow tunnel opened into a vast cavernous room made of steel and concrete.

An enormous silver train ran through the center of it on tracks that disappeared into the distance. The air was stuffier in the great cavernous room than the air outside, and the whole place was filled with people rushing by or milling about impatiently, reading books and newspapers, or peering into glowing metal rectangles they held in their hands. Bernard had never seen anything like it in his life. Animals moved among the people unnoticed, or maybe noticed but unbothered. Groups of mice dressed in gray flannel suits and holding briefcases rushed past; swallows hopped along the platform or perched on the girders that crossed the high ceiling and spoke in their clipped melodic voices to one another; rats wearing hard hats, yellow vests, and muddy work boots sat waiting for the train, snacking on sunflower seeds. It was like a whole city underground.

"Are these the people who really run the city?" Bernard asked.

Mittens laughed. "No. They're underground, all right—but these are just people going to work."

In the middle of the station, someone had drawn a circle with chalk, and a group of bugs had gathered there. They were wearing shiny black shoes that clicked when they walked, bow ties, and white gloves. Another group of bugs sat just outside the circle in little folding chairs, musical instruments in hand. One of the bugs in the band began pounding out a beat on the drums, *bump bump bump buh buh buh buh-bump*.

Three more stood up and began playing their trombones.

The bugs were the color of a penny and shaped like ginger candy, and their long antennae seemed to bounce along with the beat. A couple of them shuffled their wings and resettled them before picking up clarinets and beginning to play.

"Oh boy," Sophie said. "I love these guys."

The tallest of the bugs took off his top hat and set it on the ground at the edge of the circle. He raised his little cane in the air. "Hit it!" he cried.

Suddenly the entire horn section began to blare out a melody. Bernard's fur stood on end—the loud sound echoed in the big station, and though he was deep underground, the music made him feel like he was standing in the bright sun.

Five bugs scuttled into the chalk circle and started to dance, tap-tap-tapping out their own kind of music with their fancy shoes.

"Who are they?" Bernard asked Mittens. "What are they doing?"

"*They,*" said the cat, "are cockroaches, and *that* is tap

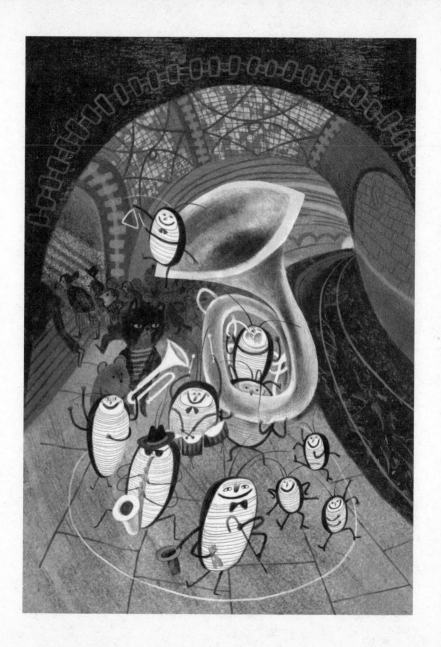

dancing. You never seen it before? Boy, Bernard, you been missing out."

Many small creatures had gathered at the outskirts of the chalk circle to hear the band and watch the dancers. There was a fat pigeon wearing a seersucker suit and a flamboyant paisley tie, a group of young mice in school uniforms, a Chihuahua dragging a leash behind him, and some moths getting an aerial view of the show. There was a nervous squirrel who had been looking for the exit but was captivated by the dancers and decided to stay; a mouse wearing a grass skirt and sparkly red shoes; and beside him four little sparrows who hopped from foot to foot, staring intently at the bugs with their shining dark eyes. Even some of the rats in hard hats pricked up their ears at the sound of the music.

The bug who had been wearing a top hat began to sing while three other bugs danced around him, acting out a story. This is what he sang:

She was smart and she was neat, she often walked
   on just two feet
The girl from the silverware drawer
She slept in a spoon, could carry a tune, and knew how
   to run when they brought out a broom
The girl from the silverware drawer

Oh, how she ran when they turned on the lights
Back to the darkness to take in the sights
Dining on cake crumbs and other delights
The girl from the silverware drawer

Oh, how she laughed when they stood on their chairs
Screaming like campers who'd just seen a bear
She danced round their feet while they pulled out
   their hair
The girl from the silverware drawer

She was brave and she was strong, she ate toothpaste
   all night long
The girl from the silverware drawer
She talked to cats, never thought about the past.
   She could even survive a nuclear blast!
The girl from the silverware drawer
The girl from the silverware drawer
The girl from the silverware drawer

The moths flew down and dropped their spare change in the top hat and then fluttered off up into the lights. The birds hopped along and dropped some crumbs into the hat, nodding at the performers and cocking their heads in appreciation. All the while people came and went on the big trains, smiling as they went past or not noticing at all.

The roaches wiped the sweat from their brows. "Thank you, thank you," they called out to the audience.

They threw kisses to the crowd as they packed up their instruments.

"Thank you, moths and squirrels, cats and mice, birds and rats," the bandleader said. "Every little bit helps. We've been rehearsing our show in subway stations for a whole year, but soon we're going to make it to Broadway! Today Delancey Street station, tomorrow the world!"

Suddenly a train rushed in, sending the remaining cockroaches skittering across the platform and nearly sweeping Bernard off his feet. The doors snapped open and what seemed like hundreds of people pushed out of the train and onto the platform.

"Hurry up," Sophie called.

Bernard scurried between many long legs and hard shoes, making his way onto the train. People sat on light blue benches on either side of the aisle. Sophie, Mittens, and Bernard sat in a corner of the train, staring at a sea of shoes and bags and packages. Then the doors snapped shut and the train took off down the tracks, deeper into the tunnel. Bernard looked around to see if the cockroaches had boarded the train, but they were nowhere to be seen. He hummed their beautiful song to himself and wondered where they got such fancy shoes.

He was feeling happy and content with the speed of the train and the company of his new friends. Then, just as he was about to ask Mittens about the shoes, he caught sight of them—there were four this time—slouching, squinting creatures with pale fur and round bellies, all wearing pork pie hats. One of them was eating a pickle. They looked Bernard up and down, smirking. One of them carried what looked like a tiny guitar case; the three others carried spears. All of them wore knives tucked into their belts.

Bernard's heart thumped in his chest.

"Mittens," Bernard whispered.

"Yeah, I see them," said the cat. "Don't let them near

you. And lissen, if we get separated, go to the Empire Diner. Can you remember that?"

"The Empire Diner," Bernard repeated.

"Dat's right," Mittens said. "In Chelsea. If you can't find us, you go there! The queen will know what to do."

♣ ♥ **6** ♦ ♠

Stand Clear of the Closing Doors

The train lurched forward and Bernard went careening across the car. He bounced off a smooth metal pole and skittered over someone's black leather boot, landing at the feet of the Pork Pie Gang.

"I see you're new in town," said the ugliest creature Bernard had ever seen. Bernard couldn't for the life of him figure out exactly what this animal was. A dog? A weasel? A big rat? There was no way to know and he was too dazed from being bounced around the subway car to speak.

"Looks like the cat's got his tongue." This time it was the one with the pickle in hand who spoke. He grinned, and his teeth were absolutely, perfectly straight. Bernard had never seen such straight teeth in all his life and there was something terrifying about it.

Bernard looked through the crowd to see if Mittens and Sophie were nearby, or at the very least to catch their eyes, but they were nowhere to be found. He tried calling out to them, but the only one who seemed to hear was a man standing above him. The man looked down at Bernard and screamed, "Help, it's a mouse!" The woman sitting next to the man took out one of the metal rectangles and held it in front of Bernard. A flash of light came from the metal rectangle, blinding him.

The train was slowing to a halt, and through the commotion of people talking and the noise of grinding brakes, Bernard heard the voice of the train conductor on the loudspeaker. "This is Secondavenue, next stop wessfourth. Stand clear of the closing doors."

Bernard's head was starting to clear and his sight was returning. He looked around frantically. Behind him, a wall of legs and feet and shopping bags crowded his vision. The train jumped forward again and Bernard rolled quickly into the nearest gangster, who dodged him by leaping up nimbly and grabbing the seat above him. Bernard smacked into the wall and stuck there with the force of the train's motion.

The subway car was slowing down once more.

"Wrap him up," Bernard heard one of the gangsters say.

Then everything went black.

♣ ♥ **7** ♦ ♠

PPGP

Bernard awoke with a start. He was no longer on the train but sitting on a lumpy couch in a dimly lit room. Something dark and cold dripped from the ceiling, and the place smelled like pickles. His paws were tied behind his back. The voices of the Pork Pie Gang were all he could hear. They were talking excitedly. As his eyes adjusted to the light, he could see that beside him sat a number of small animals: a Boston terrier wearing an eye patch, a chinchilla, and a lizard with shining gold

eyes. All of them were tied with twine, like Bernard, and all of them looked miserable.

At least a dozen members of the Pork Pie Gang stood around the room drinking green drinks from small jars, sharpening their knives, and playing darts. Some of them were huddled in conversation, laughing. Bernard listened to what they were saying.

"And then," said one of the creatures, "nothing will move. The cars will stand still, the trains will stop on the tracks, the boats will rock in the waves, never reaching the shore . . ."

Everyone in the gang had the same straight teeth. All of them slouched. Bernard racked his brain, trying to figure out just what these creatures were. The word *stoat* came to mind. He'd seen stoats back in the garden, but had certainly never seen any eating pickles, or wearing a pork pie hat, or sharpening a knife. Bernard watched them intently. They walked with their hips and bellies thrust out and their noses in the air; their arms and legs were terribly short. *Weasels*, he thought. *They must be weasels.*

"There will be nowhere to run," the creature went on in a snarling voice. "Every minute will be just like the last. Nothing will grow, nothing will fade, and no one will be able to escape."

"And we'll be able to take anything we want," said another weasel.

"Like potato chips and diamond rings and fur coats," said another weasel. "And pickles and jewel-encrusted watches. We can take all the acorns from the squirrels, put the rats out on the street, and live in their fancy kingdom."

The Boston terrier growled a little and shifted on the couch, trying to get comfortable.

The lizard had a grave, intelligent face. Bernard could tell she was listening to the weasels too.

"Did they catch you on the train?" Bernard whispered.

"I broke out of an aquarium uptown," the lizard said, keeping her voice low. "I'd made it about six blocks before one of these . . . whatever they are . . . caught me."

"That's awful," Bernard said.

"It's terribly ironic," said the lizard. "I was running for freedom—now I'm here."

The dog looked over at them and made a shushing sound.

The lizard ignored him. "I'm Ivy," she said.

"I'm Bernard," said Bernard. "I was running for freedom too."

"Oh!" said Ivy. "Where did you escape from?"

"A tea party," Bernard said.

The lizard stared at him blankly with her smart gold eyes.

"You escaped from a tea party?" the chinchilla said. "I'd give *anything* to be at a tea party right now." She rolled over on her back and tried to loosen the twine around her wrists with her feet. Beads of sweat had formed on her brow. She had a lovely thick coat of soft gray fur.

The weasels milled around the room, drinking their drinks and sharpening their weapons. If the gang kept ignoring them, Bernard thought, they could gnaw through the twine that bound one another and run for help. He looked over at Ivy, who seemed to be thinking the same thing. She stood a little closer to him.

Suddenly a door to the street opened and the room was flooded with light. More weasels slunk into the room, a whole crowd of them, eyes squinting beneath their feathered caps. Above the door in glowing letters it read *PPGP*.

He could make out a clock on the wall—it was 1:25 p.m.

What on earth could these animals want from them? Bernard wondered. Mittens hadn't told him very much about them—just to stay away from them. But what was it they really wanted?

As if she could read his mind, Ivy said, "They're going to eat us."

"*What?*" he whispered.

"They're going to eat us," she said again. "Why else would they be keeping us here? We don't have anything to steal. Weasels eat everything. It's what they do. But first they hypnotize you by dancing. It's true. Look it up."

Bernard had no idea how he might look something like that up, given their current circumstances.

The dog began a low growl again. The steady plink-plink-plink of the drip from the ceiling was clearly driving him mad.

"They're not going to eat us," the chinchilla said. "It's worse than that. We're a captive audience."

Ivy looked up at the chinchilla and blinked.

"A what?" Bernard asked.

"A captive audience," the chinchilla said. "It's when someone makes you listen to them or watch what they're doing and you can't escape because there's nowhere else you can go, or no way to get out."

"Like school?" asked Ivy.

"Yes, exactly," said the chinchilla.

Being a captive audience sounded all too familiar to Bernard. He had been a captive audience to the Mad Hatter and the March Hare for far too long. And his only escape from that endless tea party had been dreaming.

"It happened to a cousin of mine," said the chinchilla. "The Pork Pie Gang stole him from a pet store at Union Square, brought him here, and made him listen to their songs."

"But they let him go," Bernard said hopefully.

"Oh, they let him go," said the chinchilla. "But he was never the same again. You could barely recognize him. He'd chewed off all the fur on his tail, and he had a wild look in his eyes, like he'd seen a ghost. He told us he wished they'd eaten him instead."

The dog shushed them and growled, and wriggled on the couch, trying to get free. His paws were tied tightly and he was beginning to look thirsty.

Ivy flicked her long tongue out of her mouth nervously. "How long did they hold him for?" she asked.

"That's the thing," the chinchilla said. "He had no idea. My cousin had no idea at all how long he had been gone. He told us it seemed endless. Like one minute lasted a year, and a week lasted a lifetime."

The dog whimpered.

A cold shiver went up Bernard's spine. He knew exactly what the chinchilla's cousin meant. They had to get out of there before it was too late.

The tallest, fattest weasel stood on a chair.

"Silence!" he shouted.

As if he had shouted just the opposite, the room went wild with whoops and hollers. The Pork Pie Gang stamped their feet and bashed their clubs on the floor, leaping into the air. Their eyes were wild, and they were grinning their straight-toothed grins from ear to ear.

"Silence," they chanted. "Si-lence, si-lence. Gary wants si-lence!"

Gary glared at them with dark eyes and held up his hand. All at once they stopped their yowling. A hush fell over the room and the only sound anyone could hear was the steady plink-plink-plink from the drip in the ceiling.

Gary pulled a pen from his pocket and slowly began tapping it against his teeth. It made an ominous toc-toc-toc sound, like a clock. The sound of the tapping joined the sound of the dripping. Toc. Plink. Toc. Plink. Tock. Plink.

The dog squirmed on the couch, pushing his head into the sofa cushions and whimpering.

Next the weasels started to whistle a meandering tune. It was haunting and hollow, like wind blowing through a crack in a door. The sound raised the fur on Bernard's neck.

This went on for several minutes, before the rest of the weasels took out their ukuleles. Each instrument seemed to be tuned to a different note and they began plucking and strumming in no particular key or rhythm. It sounded like dozens of children jumping on a bed with squeaky springs or opening and closing doors with rusty hinges.

Then a gang member in a purple pork pie hat, looking just as serious as Gary, stepped into the middle of the room and began to sing in a high-pitched tuneless rasp, adding her shrieking yowl to the tapping and plucking and squeaking and whistling.

Zooba zooba zooba zooba zooba zooba zay
I ate at the diner the other day
I lost the buttons on my coat
I went bowling with a stoat

I punched a hamster in the throat
I threw a captain off a boat
I fed a horse some poison oats
And buttered jam and moldy toast
And then went surfing on the coast
And ate a lamb and seven roasts
And fifteen cats and a bar of soap . . .

This was too much. Unable to control himself any longer, the Boston terrier started to howl at the top of his lungs.

The lizard looked from side to side with her big golden eyes, searching for a way out of the Pork Pie Gang's lair.

Bernard watched the clock in terror as the second hand stayed right where it was. He counted. One. Two. Three. Four. Still the second hand didn't move.

The weasels applauded and laughed in delight at the

pain their song was causing. Bernard and Ivy exchanged a look. And he could see they were thinking the same thing: these creatures meant to harm them. Now they were truly running out of time. The dog continued to howl and howl as the Pork Pie Gang closed their eyes and played their ukuleles with abandon.

I have to stop them, Bernard thought. Using his sharp teeth, he began gnawing through the twine that tied the chinchilla's paws. Once free, she untied Ivy, who quickly ran over to comfort the dog. Then, working as fast as she could, the chinchilla untied Bernard.

Without a second thought, Bernard ran straight for Gary, grabbed the cuff of his pants, and swung himself around, scurrying quickly up Gary's leg until he reached his shoulder. Then he jumped into the air and, with one swift kick, knocked the pen from his hand, sending it clattering across the floor.

The toc-toc-tocking stopped; the ukulele players

stopped plucking; the singer stopped singing; the dog stopped howling; and the hands of the clock started moving once again. For one second all they could hear was the drip-drip-drip from the ceiling, before the entire room exploded in turmoil.

♣ ♥ **8** ♦ ♠

Bernard Breaks Free

Gary swiped at Bernard with his sharp claws, but Bernard ducked and then dove from the weasel's shoulder. He landed on the back of the Boston terrier, who raced for the door, winding his way between the short legs of the Pork Pie Gang and dodging blows from their heavy clubs.

The lizard, who had climbed up the wall, was now running along the ceiling upside down. The chinchilla had curled herself into a ball along the baseboard unnoticed.

They all reached the door at the same time and Bernard jumped from the terrier's back to grab the door handle, yanking it with all his might, but it was locked.

The Pork Pie Gang was closing in.

Bernard tried again—this time with the chinchilla's help. She leapt on top of the handle and pushed with her strong arms while Bernard pulled. Still nothing. The terrier scratched frantically at the door and began to cry.

Ivy stuck to the wall upside down, watching the weasels close in.

"I'll take care of this," she said calmly. She crawled into the keyhole and the animals heard several clicks and scratches; then the door opened with a pop. She had picked the lock!

The bright light of day and sounds of traffic flooded the dark room and the animals all burst out into the sunshine, Bernard and the lizard riding the dog's back and the chinchilla running along the curb with her hand in the air calling, "Taxi! Taxi!"

The weasels stumbled out on the street after them, squinting in the afternoon sun, but they were too late. A yellow taxi pulled over to the curb at Spring Street and the animals leapt inside.

The cabdriver wore a wool hat. He had glasses and big brown eyes.

He pulled back into the flow of traffic and drove several blocks before turning around to address the chinchilla.

He said, "Where you going, ma'am?"

Bernard spoke up before she could say anything. "The Empire Diner in Chelsea," he said.

The driver turned around, looking confused.

"I'm sorry, ma'am, I didn't hear you. There's some squeaking coming from the back seat. Oh, and that's a lovely coat, by the way."

The chinchilla looked up and started to speak. That's when the taxi driver stepped on the brakes. The car screeched to a halt by the side of the road, sending the animals tumbling over one another.

"This is the *fifth* time this week I picked up a chinchilla in SoHo!" said the driver. "Look, I don't mean no disrespect. But if you can't pay with cash or a credit card, and I can't *understand* you, I can't get you where you're going. Nothing personal, but . . ." He reached across the back seat and opened the door. "Out!"

Bernard, the chinchilla, the dog, and the lizard hopped out onto the sidewalk, where they were nearly crushed by two men in business suits in a great rush to get into the cab. The animals watched as the taxi pulled away and sped up Third Avenue, joining a sea of traffic that seemed to flow endlessly through the corridor of steel-and-concrete buildings.

Bernard stood for a minute to take in his surroundings. This part of the city was different from

Mittens's neighborhood, and from the subway. In Mittens's neighborhood everyone was working; here everyone seemed to be relaxing.

There were birds congregating by the curbside, and rats and mice sharing a picnic lunch. Two young starlings were painting pictures on the side of a building. A pigeon paced back and forth, checking his watch. He looked up with smiling eyes as his friend landed on a street sign and then swooped down to give him a peck on the cheek. The two of them cooed as they walked slowly across the Bowery. The block was packed with different kinds of creatures, all living side by side. You would think in such a place it would be simple to get a cab.

"Why couldn't the driver understand us?" said Bernard.

"Probably because of your accent!" said the chinchilla.

"What accent?" he asked.

"He didn't understand us because he's human," said Ivy. "They don't understand much."

This came as a shock to Bernard. "Where I come from, all creatures speak the same language," he said.

"All the creatures in England speak the same language?" said the chinchilla.

"Where's England?" Bernard asked.

"So that's not an English accent?" said Ivy.

"What accent?" he said.

Bernard's new friends stared at him for a moment. Then the chinchilla shrugged and changed the subject.

"Well, accent or no accent, he should have given us a ride," she said. "I actually *do* have a credit card, you know." She pulled a yellow-and-blue card from her thick fur coat and showed it to the other animals.

"Um. Yeah," said Ivy. "That's a MetroCard. It's for riding the subway."

The chinchilla looked at the card. The word *MetroCard* was clearly printed across the front.

"You need a card to ride the subway?" the chinchilla asked.

The dog sat on the sidewalk and scratched his head. Then he headed west at a brisk trot toward the Hudson River, leaving Bernard, the chinchilla, and the lizard behind.

"Well," the chinchilla said, "it's been nice, but I think he's got the right idea. I better be going myself."

"Wait!" said Bernard. "We can't just go back to what we were doing. We have to warn people about the Pork Pie Gang."

"I got places to be," said the chinchilla. "That was an hour of my life I'll never get back."

"Time is relative," Ivy said.

"What are you talking about?" said the chinchilla.

"Time is not a universal measurement," said Ivy. "Look it up."

"Well, it was nice meeting you, Bernard," said the chinchilla, shaking Bernard's paw.

"Wait!" said Bernard. "These weasels are dangerous. We can't let them keep playing those songs. I'm telling you, something terrible could happen."

But even as he was saying this, he wondered if it was really true. Nothing had changed out in the world. There were people everywhere going about their day. Cars zooming by; men and women walking fast, carrying packages and bags; window washers working on tall buildings; and construction workers digging deep underground.

Bernard knew this same motion and commotion was happening on every street and every block, not just in one small corner of the city—New York was filled with busy people and animals, each one with their own life. Maybe New York was too big for anyone to stop it. Out in the enormous city, his triumph in knocking the pen from Gary's hand and their brave escape now seemed small. Just one simple thing that happened in that moment—not a battle against evil. And now the Pork Pie Gang was nowhere to be seen, having given up the chase when the friends had gotten in the cab.

Still, the memory of time standing still chilled Bernard to the core.

"I know it looks like everything is fine," Bernard said, "and they're not chasing after us right now. But did you forget what happened in there?"

"No, but I'd like to," said the chinchilla as a cool breeze rippled through her fur and sent a plastic bag whirling and fluttering along the street.

"Listen," said Bernard. "I have some friends who are trying to fight the Pork Pie Gang. They told me to meet them at the Empire Diner. The queen will be there and we can listen to their plan."

"Can't do it," said the chinchilla. "I've got to pick up my laundry."

Bernard and the lizard looked at her.

"What?" she said. "You think I walk around naked like this all the time?"

"Please," said Bernard. "Remember what happened to your cousin? That could happen to all of us. The whole city. It could be teatime on Sunday afternoon forever."

"That really doesn't sound so bad," said Ivy.

"Believe me," Bernard said, "it is! What if the cars stopped moving and the trains stopped running and everyone stayed right where they were?"

"Would we still be able to eat?" the chinchilla asked.

"Yes," Bernard said. "But—"

"It sounds fine," the chinchilla said. "Goodbye, Bernard. Goodbye, Ivy. I'm going to go see what I can buy with my credit card."

♣ ♥ **9** ♦ ♠

Dinner in a Forest of Stars

Bernard and Ivy watched the chinchilla walk down the street, waving her hand in the air, trying to hail another cab.

The Dormouse and his new friend turned and headed north, keeping an eye out for members of the Pork Pie Gang. They passed a congregation of pigeons who had gathered to talk on the steps of a church; some sightseeing squirrels carrying binoculars; two young rats just leaving a dance lesson carrying their ballet shoes over their shoulders; and a starling painting the word *starling* on a parked van.

On the northeast corner of the street, there was a wrought iron fence protecting a little garden of trees and flower beds. Bernard and Ivy were about to turn the corner when they were startled by a whistle from above.

Bernard looked up, then gave a sharp cry of relief. Sitting in the branches of a sycamore tree in the little corner garden was a cat with a toothpick in his mouth.

"Mittens!" Bernard shouted.

"Bernard!" shouted the cat, breaking into a big grin. "Buddy, you okay? I seen them pickle eaters grab you on the train, so I got off at the next stop. I been looking all over for you!"

Mittens jumped down from the tree, landing gracefully in front of Bernard and Ivy.

"Pleased to meet you," he said, politely shaking Ivy's hand. "Name's Mittens."

"I'm Ivy," Ivy said.

"We're okay," Bernard said. "We managed to escape. But the Pork Pie Gang . . . It's worse than you think!"

Bernard and Ivy told Mittens about the terrible song and their narrow escape from the Pork Pie Gang Place.

"This ain't good," said Mittens. "You ain't the only ones they've been playing their crummy songs for. I been hearing stories around the bodega for weeks now."

"What we need," said Ivy, "is a coherent strategy, or at the very least a good escape plan."

Mittens looked at Ivy. He said, "This lizard is smart, Bernard."

"And she's good at picking locks," Bernard said. Ivy winked at the cat.

"All right," said Mittens. "We gotta get up to the diner so you can tell the queen what happened. If there's a whatchamacallit—a strategy—she'll have it."

At the mention of the queen, Bernard felt a little shock of fear. If this queen was like the one he had known back home, she would surely be able to rid New York of the Pork Pie Gang. He just hoped she wasn't the kind who also wanted to rid New York of lizards and mice.

As the three friends talked, a squirrel holding a blue-and-white paper cup peered at them over the top of a garbage can on the corner.

"Mittens," the squirrel called out. "Hey, Mittens. Mittens. Mittens. Mittens."

"Oh, hey, Johnny," Mittens said, looking up at the squirrel.

"Mittens," Johnny said, as though he was still trying to get the cat's attention. His black eyes were shining brightly and his paws were shaking. Mittens's ear twitched as he looked at the cup the squirrel was holding.

"Johnny, are you drinking *coffee*?" he asked the squirrel.

"Yeah, but Mittens—" the squirrel said.

"Yeah, but nothin'," said Mittens. He slapped the cup from the squirrel's paw. "You know you ain't supposed to be drinking that stuff."

"Okay, but, Mittens," the squirrel said, scrambling nervously down the side of the trash bin with quick jerky strides. "Lissen, I'm tryna tell ya. The Midtown Mice been stealing Ms. Zhang's pistachios outta the basement of the bodega again. She's asking where you are. Said she's gonna hire another cat if you don't get down there right away."

"The Midtown Mice? Are you kidding me?" said Mittens. "After all I done for those rascals? Lissen, Bernard, Ivy. I gotta get down to Ms. Zhang's. Meet you at the Empire Diner, soon as I can."

"But—" Bernard said.

"Sorry, Bernard, I ain't the kind of cat who misses a day of work."

And with that, Mittens slipped into the crowd with quick, elegant strides, until all they could see was the tip of his tail.

"I've got a feeling we might be on our own," Ivy said.

"Hey," the squirrel called to them. "Can you spare a dollah for a cup of coffee?"

Ivy and Bernard hurried on in the direction of the subway. The entrance was near a little park. Business mice and business rats sat on benches reading the newspaper, occasionally looking at their watches, but no one was coming or going on the stairs to the subway. Instead a sign was taped to the entrance saying there were no trains running that afternoon because a track was being repaired.

"We'll have to walk to Chelsea," said Bernard.

"I'll lead the way," Ivy said.

Even though he was hungry, and frightened of the Pork Pie Gang, the idea of walking through the city made him feel strong and alive in a way he had never felt back in the garden. It was strange, he thought. New York must be an enchanted place.

When Ivy and Bernard reached the sewer grate at the corner of Houston and Second Avenue, they noticed a small crowd had gathered. They pushed their way through and Bernard saw that there was another chalk circle drawn on the ground. Once again, a troupe of cockroaches scuttled out into the middle of the circle and began to dance. Tap-tap-tapping their hearts out. In the center of the circle was the bug from the subway—wearing a top hat.

"Good afternoon, ladies and gentlemen, rats and mice, sparrows and pigeons," he said. "We'd like to perform a little song for you from our musical *The Girl from the Silverware Drawer*. We've been working on this show for quite some time now. And here to sing for you is the Girl from the Silverware Drawer herself, Skippy Waterburg!"

The little crowd jostled to get a better look at Skippy. She was tall and elegant, with long antennae and soulful dark eyes. Skippy began clapping her hands in time with the tap dancers. Then she ran and twirled and skidded into the center of the circle, where she began to sing in a low, melodic voice.

The city is mine!
Every crevice and every crack
Every crumb, every snack
Every half-eaten flan is part of my plan
The city is mine, it's mine

Out of the lamplight and into shadows
Singing on street corners, talking to sparrows
Dancing at midnight and drinking espressos
The city is mine, it's mine
Basements and rooftops and high water towers
Sidewalks and streetlamps and bouquets of flowers

Out on the pavement for hours and hours
The city is mine, it's mine
The food here is divine
Pho and masala, a slice for a dollah
dim sum and sushi, a pineapple smoothie
The city is mine, it's mine
The bridges and trains, the sun and the rains
The barges and parks and each dog that barks
All of it sings like a song in my heart
The city is mine, it's mine!

Skippy glided gracefully, using her wings to flit about, and then, landing on only two feet, she took a deep bow, her antennae touching the sidewalk. She was marvelous.

"Brava!" cried the bugs in the crowd.

"Brava!" cried the pigeons and starlings.

"Encore!" called a group of young rats.

A crow hopped down from a street sign, carrying

a tiny fur coat in its beak, and gave it to Skippy, who slipped it over her shoulders.

"Thank you," Skippy said graciously.

"Thank you, everyone!" shouted the bandleader. "Let's hear it for Skippy! You can catch us again later today beneath the hot dog vendor in Washington Square Park! And tonight we're playing on the steps of the Metropolitan Museum. Tell your friends!"

Then he gave a shrill whistle and the band began packing up their instruments. All of them—the horn section, the drummer, the bass player, the bandleader, and Skippy—slipped down into the darkness of the sewer grate and disappeared.

Just as quickly as the crowd had formed, it vanished, animals all heading in different directions, going about their day.

The bright light of afternoon was beginning to fade to a clear pale blue, and the sun shone orange in the west. It made the buildings gleam and set down a shimmering path of light and shadow along the grid of streets. The windows twinkled with the lights from people's homes—so many different people, doing so many different things. Reading or cooking or painting or talking, thinking or kissing or dancing or sleeping. It was beautiful. A whole village full of people cozy in one tall building—alone and together, looking out into their speeding city at dusk.

Bernard had been in New York for just one day, but already he felt like he'd learned more than he had in one hundred years in the garden.

"Do you think we can make it to Chelsea before dark?" Bernard said.

"No," said Ivy. "It's north of here—over by the other river. It will take some time."

Ivy shivered as she talked and Bernard noticed that she was moving very slowly.

"Are you all right?" he asked.

Ivy smiled a little, then shook her head. "No, Bernard. You see, lizards are cold-blooded. We need heat from the outside to live. My aquarium had a heater in it and I didn't know New York could get this cold in the evening."

"I had no idea!" Bernard said. "Why didn't you say something sooner?"

"It's easy to forget when the sun is out and you're busy escaping from weasels," said Ivy.

"Did you always live in the aquarium?"

"No," said Ivy. "When I was young I lived in Louisiana. That's where I was hoping to go when I left the aquarium."

"Here," Bernard said to Ivy. "Climb up around my neck. Let my fur keep you warm."

Ivy walked up Bernard and wound herself around him like a scarf. Resting her head on top of his like a cap. He could feel her cold skin against him and he walked fast—hoping they could find somewhere warm before it was too late.

The streets of New York City were crowded with people, and with all kinds of creatures, headed out for dinner. Many of them sat at little tables right on the sidewalk, eating and drinking. The air was full of wonderful smells—not wonderful like the smells of Mittens's neighborhood, but the distinct smell of melting cheese and baking bread and delicious soup and herbs. Bernard's stomach growled and his mouth began watering. He also smelled pastry. A sugary buttery chocolaty smell that seemed to be coming out of a vent at the back of a restaurant.

The two friends stopped outside a tall window to look in. The place was dim and crowded, lit with tiny Christmas lights, and the people inside had big lovely meals placed before them.

Bernard followed his nose to the back of the building. A woman in an apron stood outside holding a cup like the one Johnny the Squirrel had been drinking from. She had long brown hair and beautiful pictures of mermaids and fish and ocean waves drawn on her arms. Directly behind her were three large garbage bins. Bernard could smell the food in the bins.

"Well, hello," the woman said.

Bernard looked around to see who she was talking to.

"Hello, little mouse," she said, and started laughing. "Oh my goodness! What are you doing with that lizard?"

"Hello," Bernard said. Happy to have found a person who could talk with them. "My friend is cold, and we're quite hungry."

The woman didn't respond. She didn't seem to know he was talking to her at all. She just kept laughing, then she crouched down in front of him and took out one of the rectangles all the people seemed to carry and pointed it at him—just like the people on the subway had.

"Amazing," the woman muttered. Then she tossed her coffee cup in the garbage bin and went back inside the restaurant.

Ivy had warmed up a bit, but both of them were growing hungry and tired.

"I'm going to see what else is in that bin," Ivy said, unwinding herself from around his neck and walking slowly up the side of a garbage can. "Keep a lookout."

Bernard kept watch and listened as Ivy clunked around inside the garbage can.

A few minutes later her head popped up from the top of the bin. She was holding a small white container.

He knew what was inside even before she slid down the side of the garbage can and popped it open. It was half a wheel of Camembert cheese and the heel of a baguette.

Bernard whooped for joy at their good luck. The two sat by the back door, listening to the sound of conversation and music coming from the restaurant as they had a feast of bread and cheese.

By the time they were finished, the night sky was dark as could be and the lights from the buildings glowed all around them like they were standing in a garden of stars.

Bernard's wishes had come true. He had made new friends; he had lived a whole day, hour by hour—from morning to sunset. He had eaten more than toast and tea, watched tap dancers, ridden a train underground, escaped from gangsters, and walked through a city, without falling asleep once. But now he was very tired—and worried about Ivy, who stood frozen like a statue.

Suddenly he heard a scrabbling, scratching noise coming from inside the garbage bin.

"Oh no," whispered Ivy. "They've found us."

♣ ♥ **10** ♦ ♠
A Close Call

A pointed, whiskered face stared over the edge of the garbage can. And then the animal leapt down to the alleyway, landing with a thump in front of them.

Bernard and Ivy found themselves staring into the face of a very large rat. His fur was sleek and he was dressed all in black and wore black boots. His eyes gleamed, reflecting the light from the streetlamps.

They didn't have time to run before the rat was upon them. He scooped up the lizard and shoved her into the pocket of his trousers. Bernard could see the fear in her big gold eyes.

"Stop!" said Bernard.

"Hush," the rat said. "Keep quiet." He pressed his back against the side of the building and motioned for Bernard to do the same. They kept completely still, the rat holding his finger to his lips. And then Bernard saw them: shadows slinking along the street in the lamplight. The feathered hats were unmistakable. And the figures were carrying ukulele cases. Bernard could even hear the singer muttering *zooba zooba zooba zooba zay* under her breath—like she was repeating a terrible incantation.

Then two members of the gang stopped near the alleyway. They pointed their noses in Bernard's direction and raised their heads to sniff the air. It was Gary and the singer whose terrible screeching voice had made them so miserable.

The rat raised his hand for Bernard to keep still, and they all held their breath. Waiting.

"What is it?" Gary asked the singer.

"Rats," she said. "Probably out hunting. It smells like a whole kingdom of them."

Gary squinted down the alleyway. "I don't see anything."

"And that lizard," the singer said, and shuddered. "I can smell her too, the one who unlocked the door."

Bernard stayed completely still—not daring to breathe.

They sniffed at the air for another minute, baring their terrible straight teeth.

"Don't worry," Gary said. "Soon they'll have nowhere to hide. And the city will be ours."

Then the weasels moved on, their shadows growing longer as they headed north, into the night. Bernard exhaled.

"Follow me," the rat said. "I don't have time to explain." But Bernard had no intention of letting another animal capture them.

"No!" he said. "Let go of my friend!"

"Not a chance," said the rat. "I'm not leaving this lizard out here to freeze." And with that he ducked quickly into a hole at the back of the restaurant.

Bernard chased after him. The smells of pastry and chocolate wafted from somewhere deep in the building. The hole led to a tunnel. Unlike the one he had traveled in that morning with Sophie and Mittens, this tunnel was warm and dry, and it was lined with small flickering candles. It was big enough for a cat or a small dog to travel through comfortably.

"Stop!" Bernard called after them, but the rat only ran faster, and soon, as if by magic, he disappeared altogether.

Before he could wonder what happened, Bernard felt the floor give way beneath his feet and found himself tumbling down a long metal chute. He whizzed along surrounded by darkness until he finally landed with a plop on an old feather bed.

When he looked up he saw that he was in a grand hall. The entire room was lit by candles and lanterns. Bookshelves lined the walls, and there was a long wooden table cluttered with maps and papers, some of them spilling off onto the floor. From beyond the great hall, Bernard heard the sounds of creatures talking in many different accents.

The rat turned and looked down at Bernard. He was bigger than them, and stronger, and had teeth that looked like they could gnaw through a metal drainpipe. But Bernard could also see that the rat hadn't hurt Ivy, who stood warming herself in front of the crackling fire in the fireplace. The room smelled of comfort; not just woodsmoke and books and candle wax but the earthy smell familiar to all burrowing animals, one that called to them, promising shelter.

The rat turned and looked down at Bernard; he smiled, showing his long sharp teeth.

"Welcome to the underground," he said.

♣ ♥ 11 ♦ ♠

An Underground Library

"You can't keep us here," Ivy said. The heat of the fire had given her back her strength, and she was ready to fight. But even as she said it, Bernard could see something in her that wanted to stay. He watched her eyes as she marveled at the number of books that surrounded them.

"You're right," said the rat. "I can't keep you here. I couldn't do something against another animal's wishes. If you want to leave, that hole over there leads into a bakery, and from there you can take your chances again out on the street. No one is making you stay."

Bernard remembered Mittens telling him that the people who really ran the city lived underground. He also remembered Sophie the old rat talking about eating mice as a snack. Was this rat a friend or was he trying to trick them into staying so he could snack on them later?

There is a code among small animals, the ones who know what it's like to be at the mercy of larger animals, the ones who know what it's like to be hunted, and it is this: pay attention and help one another.

Bernard and Ivy knew what it was like to be picked up and handled, carried off, stepped on; to be put in pots or aquariums; to be pinched, poked, prodded, and in Bernard's case to have hot tea poured on his nose. But if you paid attention to the details, if you stuck together, you had a chance.

"I can see the confusion on your face, my friend,"

the rat said to Bernard. "And I know one can't be too careful now with the Pork Pie Gang roaming freely. But I assure you, there's nothing to fear in the underground."

The rat opened a wooden chest in the center of the room and pulled out a feather bed and some blankets and pillows, setting them up on the rug in front of the fire.

"You'll sleep here tonight," he said. "It's been a long day, and we have a lot of work to do tomorrow."

"Tomorrow will be too late," Bernard said.

"There's time yet," said the rat. "And we're stronger together than apart."

The rat set out their bedding and blew out the candles and lanterns. Only the glow of the fire remained, casting their faces in light and shadow.

"What's your name?" Ivy called as the rat headed toward the arch, following the sounds in the distance.

He stopped and turned. "I'm Leon," he said, and smiled kindly. "Sleep well, small animals. We all need our strength."

Then he passed through the archway and slipped into the dark.

♣ ♥ 12 ♦ ♠

A Song from a Frog

Bernard woke with a start. The fire had gone out, and Ivy was nowhere to be seen. His first thought was that the day before had all been a dream. He'd spent so much of his life dreaming, back in the garden, that sometimes it was hard to tell. But this was far too real to be a dream. He was in the great hall, surrounded by books. In the daylight he could clearly see the corridor into which Leon had disappeared the night before. It was lined with paintings and photographs.

Bernard stood and stretched, then crept cautiously down the hall. Light streamed in from holes in the ceiling and shone upon the paintings that hung on either side. They were portraits of different animals. There was a painting of a crab and a tortoise, a wedding picture of two lovely young ducks hanging in a gold frame. A drawing of a dignified-looking frog wearing high rubber boots. The sounds of voices grew louder as he walked down the hallway, and the paintings seemed to stare back at him; they were pictures of squirrels and bugs and sparrows and ravens; a rabbit with a big smile on his face; a monkey wearing a party hat.

When Bernard finally stepped out of the long hallway, he found himself in a meeting room that was filled with animals as varied as the paintings on the wall. They were all talking at once.

He spotted Ivy, who was now wearing a black wool sweater and tiny wool hat. She waved to him and he hurried through the crowd to stand by her side.

Leon stood in the center of the room, waiting for the noise to die down.

"The Pork Pie Gang wants us to be their audience," Leon said. "They want us to be captives—like pets. Look at us. None of us could be pets!"

The animals all started shouting in agreement.

Leon held his paw out toward a serious-looking amphibian wearing a tweed coat. "Glub here escaped from a display of South American frogs at the Museum of Natural History! If he can break out of there, he can break out of anywhere."

The crowd clapped.

"Emma managed to get herself out of a bucket in Chinatown and walked sideways all the way from Mott Street!"

"Go, Emma!" they yelled.

"Bill left the pet store to live in the pond at Central Park FIFTY years ago."

"It took one whole year to just walk there," said Bill the turtle, whose shell was nearly as big as the table. "Everyone's in such a rush."

The crowd continued to cheer and stamp their feet.

"Ivy broke out of a tropical aquarium and weathered a harsh life on the street!" Leon said. "Cordelia and Jim might be hanging cooked and glazed in a restaurant window right now if they hadn't flown the coop. Kelly the pug? She might still be spending her days in a stupor of boredom doing tricks for biscuits."

Kelly pushed her glasses up on her face and nodded.

"And Bernard," he said. "Bernard left a . . . Bernard left a tea party."

There was murmuring from the crowd.

"But it was a very bad tea party," Bernard said. "Bad for more than a hundred years. But back where I lived, the person who stopped time did it by *accident*. He thought his song was *good*; he wasn't trying to offend Time, or anyone else. The Pork Pie Gang is stopping time *on purpose*."

"How did you get time to start again?" asked a mouse wearing a grass skirt and sparkly red shoes.

"I didn't," said Bernard. "I escaped. But back in the garden they're stuck at a Sunday afternoon tea party that will never ever end."

"Could someone *please* explain what's so bad about Sunday afternoon lasting forever?" said a hamster with cake crumbs on her face.

"Do you want to go to the park later?" Leon asked.

"Yes!" said the hamster.

"I rest my case."

"But . . ."

"Do you want to become an astronaut when you grow up?" he asked.

"Or take hula lessons!" cried the mouse in the grass skirt.

"Yes, of course," said the hamster.

"Well, these things take time," said the mouse in the grass skirt.

"Indeed they do," said Leon. "And we should all remember the song."

"What are they talking about?" Bernard whispered to Ivy.

"It's a nursery rhyme," she whispered back. "Didn't you learn it when you were a young mouse?"

Before Bernard could shake his head, Glub the frog leapt up onto the table, cleared his throat, and began to sing. He had a deep rolling baritone voice and all the creatures hushed to listen to his song.

Time: It's shaped like a coil
It tastes like tinfoil
You need it to boil an egg
or uncoil a snake from your leg
Or stand on your head

Or ride a bobsled
Or comfort a lonely chameleon named Fred
All of these things take time!

Time's not running out
It's not on your side
It shouldn't be wasted or toasted or fried
Or buttered or shuttered or pickled or dried
You need it to catch all manner of flies
All of these things take time!

Time's not in a race. It IS part of space
You need it to scrub all the dirt off your face
Or fall down the stairs or trip on a rake
Or eat chocolate ice cream down by the lake
All of these things take time!

"Does that make things clearer?" Leon asked, when the song was over.

There was a low murmuring of "I suppose," or "No, not really," or "Well . . . maybe."

"That song was ridiculous," Ivy whispered into Bernard's ear. "Time is actually part of the fundamental structure of the universe."

"It's not," said a squirrel who overheard her. "It's something made up by people."

"In any case," said Ivy, "it doesn't seem like the underground has thought this through very carefully."

"Friends," Leon said. "Before now, the Pork Pie Gang was just roaming the streets looking for animals to kidnap and turn into a captive audience. They were just practicing. But yesterday some of our mice on the inside found something much worse."

Three mice wearing black turtleneck sweaters and black boots scurried into the center of the room carrying a rolled-up poster and handed it to Leon. Leon unrolled it, revealing an advertisement. There was a picture of Gary the Weasel smiling in his pork pie hat, and beneath the picture it read:

PPGP Presents:
The First, Last, and Only Endless Ukulele Concert!
Seven o'clock on May 25 at Times Square
All are welcome.
Free pickles.

A hush fell among the animals as one by one they understood what this meant.

"They're done practicing," Leon said. "And we have to act fast. Because in just two days from today, the Pork Pie Gang will stop time for the entire city and make us all do what they do: nothing. They're a band of roving slobs, trying to push us all around and make us stop thinking. They want us to be like them, talking about pickle juice or their vacation or ukulele strings, but worst of all, they want to make it so we have no future, so we can't go anywhere to escape them."

"Got it," said Ivy, who was growing tired of speeches. "What's the plan?"

♣ ♥ 13 ♦ ♠

On the Banks of an Underground River

"We need to get to the Empire Diner!" said Bernard. "My friend Mittens is there, and Sophie, and the queen. I think they can help us."

"Mittens the mouse hunter?" Leon asked.

"What?" said Bernard. "No. It's not like that. This cat is my friend."

Several of the small animals exchanged looks. Some of the mice were trembling.

Bernard looked at Ivy and she raised an eyebrow. It was true that the last time they'd seen Mittens, he was complaining about the Midtown Mice.

"Mittens told me if we got separated to meet him at the Empire Diner," Bernard said. "He said the queen would know what to do, and I trust him."

"All right," said Leon. "We don't have much choice right now—we're running out of time. We'll have to split up. But be careful. Bernard, Ivy, and Glub, you take the crosstown ferry to Chelsea—see what you can find out. And remember if you get separated, go to the Empire Diner and wait. That goes for all of us."

Bernard and Ivy followed Glub, as he strode through the room in his high rubber boots, his nose in the air. They passed through the great hall and down a flight of steps into a dank passageway that smelled of mold. It was lit with a single lantern, and very dark.

At the end of the passageway was another flight of steps, this one lit by candlelight. The smell of mud and earth and sewer gas was all around them. And soon they could hear the sound of water rushing past. They had reached an underground river. Black water glinted in candlelight and a misty fog hung in the air around them.

On the banks of this river there was a little docking station. Some mice, dressed sharply in business suits and holding briefcases were waiting there. Several of them were reading the newspaper. One looked impatiently at his watch and then back out at the water. They didn't seem worried at all about the Pork Pie Gang—on the contrary, they didn't seem to know anything was wrong at all.

Three large water bugs were also waiting for the ferry. They were holding scripts and practicing lines from a play, saying the same words over and over, trying to get them right. Beside the bugs stood a family of rats. The mothers were reading a map together and the children were throwing stones into the river. Partway down the pier Bernard could see the cockroaches practicing another song from their show—running and jumping and tapping along, then the bandleader would clap his hands for them to stop and they'd do it all over again.

Soon they could see a large round light in the distance and then the ship appeared, speeding through the dark water and docking along the shore. The captain was a wizened toad with moles on his face. His eyes were golden like Ivy's.

The business mice boarded first, rushing on and settling themselves at tables on the upper deck. Then the mothers with children, then the cockroaches— stacking their instruments up just inside the ferry's entryway.

Glub spoke to the captain in a language Bernard didn't understand, and the old toad ushered them aboard, clapping each of them on the back with his strong hand.

The ferry set off along the river, and all along the shore, lights flickered from lanterns and small fires. Bernard could see creatures gathered there. Rats mostly, and dogs and cats who looked like they'd once been pets, along with a few thin and bedraggled racoons. Some were building shelters; others were collecting litter or cooking. A few frogs stood on the banks of the underground river in their rubber boots, fishing.

"Who are they?" Bernard asked.

"Homeless creatures mostly," said Glub.

Bernard didn't understand. It looked to him like their home was along the river.

"It's hard living for some up in the light of the city," the frog went on. "Not everyone can be a business mouse. Down here they can find shelter."

"Do they like it down here?"

"Some do; some don't," said Glub. "They don't have much choice."

Bernard thought it must be terrible to live so close to the crosstown ferry, with the dank moldy smells and the noise of the boat all day and all night. It was hard to believe this place was so close to the great hall with its crackling fire and feather beds and books, and the smell of chocolate pastry in the air.

"It must be hard not to have a home," Bernard said.

He looked at Ivy sitting on the deck, reading a book she had brought from the library underground. Something had changed about her from when he first met her in the Pork Pie Gang Place. Even though the Pork Pie Gang threatened to wreck New York, even though they had no time to spare in stopping them, even though she had nearly frozen from cold and she was no closer to Louisiana and they might all be swept up in a timeless void, Ivy seemed happier. She looked warm and content dressed in her black cap and sweater. She looked up from her book and smiled.

"Will you ever go back to your home?" Ivy asked Bernard.

The question startled him. The ship cut through the fog as it zipped along the black water beneath the tall gray city and Bernard thought for a moment of the garden. The green grass, the lovely roses, thick and lush with life. The smells of sugar and honey and scones and tea. The March Hare's quick wit. There was a time before time stopped that they were his friends. When they could visit each other freely and roam through the countryside, when they could tell each other stories or play croquet, or listen to the turtles singing by the sea. He tried to remember what home was like before that terrible song.

There was a time before time stopped that he could be alone, lie in meadows or on the beach, listening to waves crashing in. New York City was beautiful. Full as a forest, teeming with life and light and motion. But he wondered if he would ever smell roses again. And even if he wanted to go back—if he could make amends with time and get the clocks moving in the garden—how would he do it? How could he leave New York City when it had answered all his wishes? He didn't even understand the magic that had brought him there.

"I don't know if I could ever go back," Bernard said. "I guess I'm homeless too."

♣ ♥ 14 ♦ ♠

A Feast of Flowers

The ferry docked beneath a sign that read West Twenty-Eighth Street, rocking in the choppy water.

Bernard and Ivy hopped out onto solid ground and followed Glub up a long flight of stairs to street level, leaving the dark passageway behind. They came out from beneath a curb into the bright sunlight and stood stunned, staring up from the sidewalk at what looked like a jungle of flowers.

The streets were lined with color. Everywhere they looked, in front of each building there were baskets of wisteria and bouquets of roses, blue irises and long stalks of hollyhocks; blooming magnolia trees and lilac bushes and crab apples, planted in plastic pots. Men unloaded bales of cherry blossoms and baskets of peonies and bundles of tulips in every color, carrying them from refrigerated trucks that idled in the street into the shops and warehouses.

Bernard could not believe his eyes. Yellow daisies and bright red poppies, forsythia and sunflowers, dahlias and snapdragons, white lilies and frangipani and roses like he had never seen before in his life, blooming yellow and red and orange and white, pink and some so deep ruby-red they were almost black, their buds like tiny cabbages.

A breeze moved through the air and Bernard breathed in the scent of lilac and hyacinth and rose, swooning from the cool beautiful perfume of the flowers. The street smelled like a majestic rose garden in full bloom, like a rolling meadow beneath the summer sun.

Bees buzzed around from shop to shop, smelling flowers and gathering pollen. They danced with delight in front of each other—giving one another directions and sharing gossip.

Ivy climbed into a grove of tropical plants and began to bask.

"Are we still in New York?" Bernard asked.

"Of course," Glub said. He turned his head quickly and caught a fly with his tongue, then wiped his mouth with a linen handkerchief and tucked it into the sleeve of his tweed jacket. "This is the flower district."

Beneath the large stands where people shopped there were smaller stands full of the hustle and bustle of mice selling their own flowers; violets and bluebells and snowdrops and crocuses. The mice wore wool hats to keep themselves warm. The shops had to be refrigerated so the flowers would live longer. Bernard watched the strong mice carrying cases of buttercups and baby's breath. They lived, day in day out, among this beautiful feast of flowers. Bernard thought about Mittens and his many jobs in the city and wondered what a mouse had to do to find work in the flower district.

He was just imagining a life of hard work in the service of beautiful things when he heard a series of doors slam. One by one, the flower sellers on the lower level were scurrying about—pulling the flowers in from the street and shutting themselves in their shops.

Then he spotted them—slinking along, bellies and hips pushed out, noses in the air, hats pulled down over their eyes. Two members of the Pork Pie Gang were walking along snickering to each other, mocking the flowers and rolling their eyes. Bernard watched as they snapped the neck of a daisy, her head falling to the side, unable to move. The other hacked through an entire family of poppies, their delicate petals scattering to the sidewalk, their heads left bare and gray.

Without thinking, Bernard leapt in front of the weasels.

"Stop," he said.

They looked down at him with blank eyes and then laughed, showing their straight teeth.

"Who's going to stop us?" they asked. And to make her point, one of the weasels plucked a violet from its stem and popped it into her mouth. Bernard heard the violet's last gasp, a ragged tearful cry, as the weasel bit down on it and its blood stained her teeth purple.

"I will!" said Bernard.

"Look around, little creature," said the weasel with the blood of the flower on her teeth. "Do you see anyone who cares to stop us? Do you see anyone who can? Certainly not you."

Bernard knew the weasels expected him to be afraid—but the truth was, he was too angry to be afraid. He knew the weasel thought he was weak. But he had been fighting against the Hatter for his whole life—fighting against a madman—and that was far more difficult and dangerous than fighting a member of the Pork Pie Gang.

She pulled out her knife and pointed it at Bernard's chin, but he turned quick as a flash and, looping his tail around her feet, spun round, tripping her to the pavement. The other weasel watched the whole thing with a pickle sticking out of his mouth. He didn't lift a finger to help her. But Bernard's friends leapt to his side. Glub and Ivy stood ready for the weasel to attack. The mice who had been watching from inside their shops came to stand beside him too.

Suddenly the weasel didn't seem so sure of herself. She looked back nervously at the other member of the

Pork Pie Gang, who finally took out his knife.

As soon as she saw this, Ivy jumped on his back. Glub snapped off the weasel's hat with a flick of his long tongue and the pigeons who had been watching from the awnings swooped down and pecked him on the head. Bees rose up from the flowers and swarmed around him. He swiped at them and dropped the knife. Ivy kicked it into the gutter, where it fell down a sewer grate.

"You won't win!" Bernard said. "There's more of us than there are of you."

More pigeons swooped down and pecked at both the weasels. They ducked and waved their arms, striking at the birds, but the pigeons flew off beyond their reach and then the bees returned with a threatening buzz.

"We stick together," Bernard said. "You better get out of here before the rest of us show up."

The weasel spat the blood of the violet onto the sidewalk. Then the two of them put their hats back on and headed quickly up the street, away from the flower shops.

"It doesn't matter," she called back to them. "In two days you'll all be doing exactly what we want. There's no way you can stop us."

♣ ♥ 15 ♦ ♠

The Girl with the Long Blond Hair

Once the weasels were out of sight, the small creatures of the flower district let out a cheer. A handsome mouse with his whiskers cut short put a wreath of tiny flowers around Bernard's neck and gave flowers to Ivy and Glub. The bees went back to dancing and a pigeon passed around lemon candies and everyone took one—wincing at first because they were so sour but eating them anyway because they were also sweet.

"They come through here all the time," one of the shopkeepers told Bernard, the tip of his tail twitching with excitement. "And we've always shut things down. We never thought the pigeons would come and help us if we fought back."

"Of course we would," said the pigeon who had handed out the lemon candies. "The fact is, we should have done something about it long ago."

But there was little time to talk—more customers had shown up and the hustle and bustle of flower selling had begun again.

People who had stopped momentarily to watch the commotion of animals were now back to their shopping. Bernard looked up from the low stalls and watched them. They moved quickly with long strides, hailed cabs from the corner, rode past on bicycles, stuck bouquets of flowers in their bags. They all looked so busy with places to go—and yet they didn't understand the language of animals. They watched the weasels with amusement, or saw them as a nuisance, not knowing the danger they might bring.

Glub put on a pair of reading glasses and was consulting a map. Ivy was talking to a pigeon about joining the underground. Just as Bernard was about to say they should all get on their way, he saw her. Walking with her mother. The girl from the garden! She was wearing a blue dress, knee socks, and black shoes. Her long hair fell at the sides of her face as she leaned down to smell a bouquet of red carnations.

As if under a spell, Bernard slipped through the crowd and climbed up the side of the flower stall to get a better look at the girl. He watched her pull some money from her pocket and hand it to a dark-haired man wearing gardening gloves and a white smock.

It was her—he was sure of it. And surely she would be able to help them! Bernard remembered how she had tried to talk to him when he was stuck in the garden and how he kept falling asleep. He knew that she understood about the Hatter and the March Hare and about Time. She would be able to explain it to the people who couldn't understand. His heart soared.

Before he had time to regret it, Bernard hoisted himself up onto the flower stall and climbed into the pocket of the girl's skirt—keeping out of sight of her mother. People are sometimes prejudiced against mice and he didn't want to risk it.

"Bernard," called Ivy, "have you lost your mind?"

"I'll be back soon," he called to her.

"Bernard," Glub called, "get down from there! What are you doing?"

"I'm getting us more help!" he said. "We'll meet you at the Empire Diner."

The girl took her bouquet of carnations and slung a backpack over her shoulder and headed through the market. Now Bernard could see the street from up high at pocket height. It was quite a different way to see the world.

The girl and her mother walked along the bustling Chelsea street until a yellow cab stopped and they got in. The car was cool inside and the smell of the carnations suddenly filled his nostrils and soon he was very tired. The motion of the cab and his cozy place inside the pocket made him feel safe and free from worry. The Pork Pie Gang's plan seemed like a distant memory. It had been a long time since he felt the pull of dreams so heavy on his eyelids. He hunkered down in the pocket and fell fast asleep.

Bernard awoke to a large hand clutching his body and a startled yelp. He had hoped he might climb out of the pocket on his own when they reached her house, but now she was lifting him in the air, holding him level to her face so that they could look into each other's eyes. Her skin was pale and smooth and her eyes were a deep gray-blue, like a stormy sea, and sparkled smartly.

"Hello, little mouse," she said. Just like the woman

outside the restaurant had said to him. But she didn't take out a rectangle and flash a light in his eyes. She just looked at him.

"Hello," he said.

The girl's room was large and airy. The flowers she had bought from the market smiled from a vase in the center of a small table that was set for tea. There was a pair of sneakers and a large orange ball in the corner, and an easel with a half-finished painting of a crocodile on it. The walls were painted pale blue.

"What's your name?" she asked—and for a moment he wondered if he had gotten it all wrong and she was just talking to herself, like the woman in the alley had been. Maybe she was trying to figure out what she might call him.

"Bernard," said Bernard.

"That's a very nice name," said the girl, and Bernard looked at her in awe. She could understand every word he said!

"I don't meet many mice with names like that," she said.

"Do you know many mice?" Bernard asked. It seemed to him she must—as she could communicate very well, no hint of an accent.

The girl nodded. "My mother is a professor, and there are many mice that help her with her work. Sometimes I get to bring one home!"

Bernard had never heard of mice working with professors, but it seemed like a good job and he knew that mice and college professors often dressed alike and had similar habits.

"What's your name?" Bernard asked the girl.

"Allie," she said.

She set him on the windowsill. And from her window he could see down to an enormous lawn. It was incredible—a lush place enveloped in a canopy of green that stretched for blocks and blocks. It was full of paths and ponds and large boulders and was surrounded on all sides by towering buildings that shone in the sun. Bernard had never seen anything so beautiful. It was as though the hard, fast city opened up at its center to reveal the loveliest garden. He was speechless.

"Is that your garden?" Bernard asked.

The girl laughed. "It's everybody's garden," she said. "It's Central Park."

Bernard looked out at the park and the tall buildings. He watched birds diving from the window ledges, swooping down into the green. They looked majestic and brave.

"What are those birds?" Bernard asked.

"They're falcons," she said. "They nest up here in the high-rises because it reminds them of mountains."

Allie's view of the city made it seem like a different world, and her room was so cozy he almost forgot why he had wanted to talk to her.

"Do you remember me?" he asked.

The girl shook her head. "I'm afraid I can't really tell

one mouse from another," she said. "I don't mean to be rude."

"But you can understand me."

"Of course," said the girl, "I'm not a barbarian."

Bernard thought there must be something a little magic about her. Even though she didn't recognize him. "Allie," he said, "I need your help. There is a group of weasels called the Pork Pie Gang and they are trying to stop time."

The girl smiled and knelt near the windowsill so she could be closer to him.

"Tell me more!" she said.

"My friends and I are going to meet the queen at the Empire Diner and we are going to fight them."

The girl laughed and stroked his fur lightly with her index finger. "This is wonderful."

Bernard was glad she thought so—she must know exactly what to do.

"Mice have the best stories!" she said.

"It's not a story," Bernard said. "It's real."

"That's even better," said Allie. "What happened next?"

"No, it's—" Bernard began, but he didn't have time to finish his sentence. There was a knock at the door and Allie turned from the window and stood in front of Bernard, blocking him from view.

The girl's mother leaned her head in; she was wearing a sweater and had long brown hair and thick glasses. She said, "Allie, we've got to get going; our reservation is for six o'clock."

When she closed the door, Allie turned back to Bernard.

"I'm sorry, I have to leave you for a bit," she said.

"No, wait!" said Bernard.

"We'll talk more when I get back," said Allie. Then she picked him up gently and carried him over to a small cage on top of her dresser—opened the top and dropped him inside.

♣ ♥ 16 ♦ ♠

Free Birds and Trapped Mice

The cage was filled with cedar chips and he could smell the animals who had lived there before him. It was a smell of half-eaten scraps and frightened mice.

The girl did not come back until it was dark. While she was gone Bernard walked around the cage, poking his head out and trying to see the park. He could see just a sliver of sky out the window—every once in a while, one of the fast, graceful birds whizzed past. He watched as one settled on the window ledge. The bird

was very large, dark gray with a white belly, a small hooked bill, and yellow rings around its black eyes. Its talons were large and looked strong and sharp. The bird seemed lost in thought.

While the sun was still shining through the window, he looked around her room. Her bed was big and covered with a pale blue comforter with pictures of clouds on it. He looked at the table and tea set. The teapot was blue and white like the one they had used in the garden. But the picture on the side was different. On this teapot there was a picture of a long table in the center of a garden; a rabbit and a mouse sat on either end of the table and a man in a top hat sat in the middle.

Bernard rubbed his eyes and looked again. Could it be true? Was this a picture of the garden? He sat in the cage, wondering how she could have found such a teapot, and how he could get out to inspect it more closely. He tried everything he could to unhinge the lock on the top of the cage. What had he done? He had left his friends and now he was stuck.

He hung with all his strength on the bars of the cage, trying to pick the lock with his long fingers and then with his tail. If only Ivy were there to help him. He called out to any other mice that might be hiding in the room, but it was no use. Silence reigned in the clean, beautiful space, and he sat alone and afraid until the light faded to darkness.

After a time he heard the door open, and then Allie came straight to him and opened the cage.

"Sorry I was gone so long," she said. "We went to a show after dinner."

She lifted him out and placed him on the table, putting a little package in front of him on a tiny plate.

"This is onigiri," she said. "I think you'll like it."

Inside the package was a ball of rice wrapped in a dark green leaf. It smelled delicious; sweet and savory and like the sea. Bernard bit into the strange food. Inside there were green vegetables and sesame seeds. He devoured it.

"Will you tell me the rest of the story now?"

"It's not a story, Allie. It's important that we meet my friends and that we tell people what they are planning. We don't have much time. I thought you could help me, but if you can't, can you please let me go?"

"I can help you," said Allie. "You can live with me here and be my pet."

Bernard felt his heart sink.

"Allie!" he said. "I can't do that. I live in the world, not in a cage. And I have to get to my friends—to help them fight the Pork Pie Gang."

She looked at him closely.

"I think I have some clothes that will fit you," she said, and pulled out a little box from her desk drawer.

Inside it there was a variety of small costumes and clothes.

She took out a mouse-sized pair of sneakers, a mouse-sized ballet costume, a mouse-sized top hat and tuxedo.

"Try on the tuxedo!" said the girl, setting the top hat on his head.

"No," said Bernard. "Allie, thank you for dinner but I need to leave. I need to meet up with my friends in the underground."

Just then the girl's mother called to her from the hallway. "Allie, lights out. It's bedtime."

"Sorry, Bernard," Allie said. "We can talk about it in the morning."

"No, no," he said. "Please don't put me back in the cage. We're running out of time!"

But she did put him back in the cage—this time setting it on the windowsill. Then she put on her pajamas and turned off the light.

Bernard gazed out over the towering skyline of New York City and down into the sparse darkness of the park, lit by the buttery glow of the occasional streetlamp. The city was magnificent. Soon there might never be another sunset, or bright lights twinkling in the darkness; there might never be another morning song on the subway, or a new delivery to the flower district, or a walk through Chinatown with Mittens.

In a day it could all be stopped—the whole city was as powerless as a mouse in a cage.

♣ ♥ 17 ♦ ♠

A Magic Teapot

In the morning the sun rose orange and gold and reflected in the windows of the buildings that surrounded the park. The bird was on the window ledge again, its black eyes scanning the city. Wind ruffled its feathers, but it seemed to feel no chill. Bernard watched the bird with longing. He banged on the side of the cage so that it might look over and see him. Next time Allie let him out of the cage, he decided, he would run.

Timelessness had been hard in the garden, but the idea of timelessness in New York City was frightening. Especially if he had to spend it inside Allie's room. No fresh air, no other animals to talk to. He wondered if Allie's teapot, like the one he had used to escape, the one with pictures of bridges on it, might lead him back to the garden. Time was running out—and it might be his only chance.

An alarm clock rang, startling Bernard. The falcon turned its head toward the window and spotted him. It nodded gravely in his direction and lifted one of its frightening talons in a kind of salute.

Allie jumped from her bed and ran straight to the cage. The bird soared off into the open air, giving a triumphant cry before swooping down into the green of the park.

"Good morning, little mouse!" Allie said as she lifted Bernard out of the cage and put him on the table in front of the teapot. He had told her his name but still she called him nothing but little mouse, as though all mice were the same.

The carnations smelled wonderful and the room was bathed in the pale glow of early-morning light. He stood inches away from the blue-and-white china teapot. Allie was too close for him to run away—he couldn't risk her catching him again and maybe keeping him in the cage all the time.

"Where did you get this teapot?" Bernard asked.

The girl smiled. "My aunt gave it to me for my birthday," she said. "It's very old, and it's very special."

Allie set out two cups, one small enough for Bernard to hold. When she opened the lid of the pot, the smell of tea and roses and milk wafted to his nose.

Bernard felt his fur standing on end—and a prickly electric feeling. As soon as she took off the lid, the pot seemed to be giving off a magnetic pull. He crept forward and climbed up the side of the pot, peering into it. To his surprise there was no tea inside, only dust and a few dried rose petals crumpled at the bottom. But the longer his head was over the rim of the pot, the dizzier he felt. Suddenly he heard a clatter of silverware and the sound of the March Hare's voice—his quick way of speaking.

The dust at the bottom of the pot began to rise and form a little cloud. In the center of that cloud he could see, as clearly as if he were looking through a window, the rosebushes, the lush green lawn, and the long table filled with scones and butter and tea. In the garden, the March Hare sat in his chair looking forlorn—peering into yet another teapot—the one with the pictures of bridges on it, the one Bernard had used to escape.

"Where is he?" the March Hare asked. "Dormouse!" he called into the teapot. "Come back." He could see the Hatter standing on the table in the middle of the cups and saucers, wearing muddy boots and leaning over the March Hare's shoulder. They were searching for him.

Bernard reached his paw deeper into the teapot and suddenly he could smell the grass of the dewy lawn and the smoke of the chimney. He reached in deeper still and touched the corner of the tablecloth, the cool smooth cotton. It was all so familiar and safe. He knew if he reached in even farther, he could go back there himself. He could leave Allie's room, leave New York and the threat of the Pork Pie Gang. He could slip back into the garden where the roses never stopped blooming. It might have been hard and dull in the garden and sometimes people hurt him—but it would be easier than this race against time and better than being trapped in Allie's room for all of eternity.

"Dormouse!" the Hatter and the March Hare called into the teapot. "Dormouse!"

Why aren't they calling me by my name? Bernard wondered, and then he remembered. They had never, in a hundred years of timelessness, known it. They had never asked. They had never assumed he had one. And he hadn't known their names either.

No, Bernard thought. It wouldn't be better to be in Allie's room—to trade one tea party for another. He thought of Mittens and Ivy and Leon and Glub and all the creatures in the underground. He thought about all the things he had seen in New York and about the boredom and sadness he felt in the garden. What he wanted most was to escape from Allie's room so he could help his friends.

And if the Pork Pie Gang got their way and time stopped, he could at least look out at the park and see the majestic birds. It would be sad but it would be better to live like that than in the middle of nowhere, where there was never a new story or song and where the people who knew him didn't know him at all.

Allie's mother called her to get ready for school. And this time the girl did not put him back in the cage.

"Wait for me here," she said. "When I come home we can have a special tea party."

"Allie," said Bernard. "There's no time for waiting and no time for tea parties. Tonight the Pork Pie Gang is going to stop time!"

"You are so funny!" she said. "I love the stories you make up." She leaned down and kissed him on the nose. "Wait for me here, then we can play more when I get home."

Then she shut the door and left him there. There was no way to creep under the door—the crack was too small—no way to lift the window; he was too weak. And no way to call for help; his voice was too quiet. But somehow, Bernard thought, somehow, he had to break free.

♣ ♥ 18 ♦ ♠

A Brave Escape

Bernard scurried up to the windowsill, climbed up the curtains, and stood on top of the window frame. There he could see that the window was locked. He braced his feet against the glass and his back against the lock. Then he pushed and heaved with all his might until he felt the lock slowly begin to give. Sweat dripped from his brow and he turned the other way— this time pushing the lock with his feet. Suddenly the lock clicked and slid easily. He had done it!

But how could he ever pry the window open? He jumped down from the windowsill and searched the room for something he could wedge beneath the window. He found a long, colored pencil that was lying beneath the easel and dragged it in his teeth up to the windowsill. Maybe he could wedge it into the bottom.

All of this commotion caught the attention of the falcon, who had settled again on the ledge outside the window. It folded its long wings and this time it stared straight at Bernard with its yellow-rimmed eyes.

"Hello!" Bernard shouted, waving at the bird and pounding on the window. "I'm trapped here."

The falcon cocked its head. Its eyes gleamed.

Bernard pointed to the top of the window frame. "I unlocked the window—but I can't get it open!"

The falcon balanced on one foot and, with its other strong talon, wrenched the window up and open. A cool breeze blew into the room and ruffled through Bernard's fur.

"Thank you!" said Bernard. "Oh, thank you."

"My pleasure," said the falcon. Her voice was clear and full like a bell. "My name is Hunter. And who are you?"

"Bernard."

"Normally, Bernard," said the falcon, "a mouse would never ask me for help."

"Oh," said Bernard. "Why is that?"

Hunter looked at him curiously, her eyes glinting as if she'd heard a joke. "Because I would eat them."

"You . . . You would . . ." Bernard was trembling, his heart pounding in his chest. "But you can't. I . . . there's, we have to . . ."

"Luckily for you," Hunter said, "I'm not hungry. I just ate a weasel."

Bernard caught his breath and put his hand on his forehead.

"At least I think it was a weasel," Hunter said. "It was wearing a little hat. Maybe it was a tiny man in a fur coat—it had very straight teeth. Quite delicious."

Bernard quickly told Hunter about the Pork Pie Gang. There were only hours left before the concert at Times Square. Now that Hunter was standing right next to him, he could see how strong she was. He could see her sharp beak and her intelligent eyes.

"So let me get this straight," said Hunter. "You and a lizard from Louisiana, and some other tiny animals, and a cat and a queen—who I've never heard of before—are going to stop a group of gangsters from making time stand still? Have I got that right? And these gangsters are weasels with little hats and straight teeth—like the tasty morsel I *just* told you about."

"I know it sounds crazy," Bernard said. "I know it sounds made up. But it's true."

"Huh," said Hunter. "And these weasel gangsters are all going to be gathering at Times Square—right in the middle of the city—tonight?"

"Yes," said Bernard. "All of them. I'm telling you the truth. It's not a story. And we'll all be there to stop them."

"Hmmm," Hunter said. "Very interesting."

She turned her back on Bernard and looked out into the blue sky, as though she were getting ready to fly away. Bernard's heart sank. Why would no one believe him? Why was it so hard for bigger animals to imagine the things that smaller animals said were true? Why was it hard for them to see the things that smaller animals saw? Why would he lie about something so important for everyone?

"Well?" said Hunter.

"Well what?" said Bernard sadly.

"Well, hop on," she said. "We have to hurry."

With an excited squeak, Bernard jumped onto the falcon's back, holding tightly to her feathers. Hunter leapt off the window ledge, into the sky, spreading her enormous wings and soaring out over the streets and the park.

The falcon caught currents of air, gliding at first and then speeding faster and faster. Faster than the cars on the road and the boats on the river and the trains underground. She circled the park, getting lower and lower. Bernard clung to her, dizzy from the speed and the height, the wind in his fur, terrified that he might fall. He thought again he must be dreaming.

As Hunter flew lower, Bernard could see there were ponds and lakes in the park, and a castle. There were people in uniform riding horses and on horse-drawn carriages, people on bicycles, families of squirrels and rabbits out having a picnic. This park was surely an enchanted place. He had only seen things like this in books or heard about them in stories. The smell of grass and trees and flowers rose into the air—and mixed with the smells of coffee and eggs coming from the vendors, and the smells of cars and buses on the street.

The falcon circled the low boulders and bridges and statues in the park, then came to rest in a tree overlooking a gleaming green pond. People rowed

boats in the late-morning sun, and others sat on benches surrounding the pond, reading newspapers.

Hunter glided gently to the ground and Bernard climbed off her back.

"This is as far as I can take you," said the falcon. "If you head south, you can get the subway to the diner."

"Thank you!" said Bernard. He hurried along the edge of the pond. Now that he was back on ground, he could see things invisible to the larger world. A group of field mice playing baseball. A forlorn rabbit sitting on the edge of the pond, in deep conversation with a frog. There was a painter—the same young starling he had seen in SoHo painting the word *starling* on a van. Now she was standing in front of an easel, painting a picture of the pond.

Several round stones stuck up out of the reedy water. Bernard decided to walk over them, cutting across the pond to save time.

He scurried across one and jumped to the next, then the next. When he got to the next one it began to move. Bernard hunkered down to get his balance, then slowly the tiny rock in front of the one he was standing on began to rise out of the water. It turned—and Bernard found himself looking into the eyes of an ancient turtle.

"Oh!" Bernard cried. "I thought you were a rock."

The turtle dipped his head a bit and raised his eyebrows. "It happens."

Bernard looked out at the other rocks. Many of them were moving—and he could see now that most of them were turtles, all different kinds of turtles.

"I didn't mean to intrude in your neighborhood," Bernard said. "Or use you like a stepping-stone. I'm in a hurry and wasn't thinking."

"I can give you a ride," the turtle said.

"Um . . ."

"I know, I know," said the turtle. "Everyone thinks we're slow as snails. I'll tell you one thing—we're not slow as snails. Snails are slower."

As he was talking, the turtle began swimming toward the other shore.

"Everyone's in such a hurry," the turtle said.

Bernard thought about jumping off his back and swimming, but it seemed rude, and anyway he didn't know if he could go much faster himself. He thought of jumping to another stone, but he might end up in the same situation, riding on someone's shell. The sky was blue and the green pond smelled of mud and algae and life. In the distance he could see above the tree line, the tops of buildings rising into the sky.

"Especially small animals," the turtle said. "Running from one place to another. Always in a rush."

"I'm in a rush today," said Bernard, "because the Pork Pie Gang is trying to stop time, and I'm trying to stop them."

"Never heard of them," said the turtle. "I've been in this pond for sixty years and never once heard of any gang."

"Just because you haven't heard of them doesn't mean they don't exist," Bernard said. He was getting tired of arguing and explaining and convincing other creatures. Time was running out and it couldn't be wasted trying to make them understand. The turtle would be no help—now it was up to Bernard to make sure the turtle didn't hold him back.

As soon as they swam close to another turtle, Bernard hopped from one shell to the next. This turtle didn't seem to know he was there at all, and when he got close to a rock, Bernard jumped again.

Now he was stranded in the middle of the pond on a jagged stone covered with grass and twigs and moss. Relying on the turtles had taken him off course. He scanned the horizon frantically and looked into the water, searching for anything or anyone that might help him get to shore.

In the distance he could see falcons circling. He waved at them and shouted for help. Like a flash a bird came down and sank its sharp talons in the moss beside him; he could smell the blood of other animals on the bird's claws. This bird meant no help at all— it was hunting for lunch. Bernard crouched in the tall grass, hiding and trembling. As fast as the bird had struck, it flew back up into the sky with a terrifying call, circling above and scanning the ground. Hunter had been right; a mouse could rarely find help from a falcon.

Bernard steadied himself and prepared to dive into the cold water. There was no other choice. At the edge of the rock he noticed the chunk of moss the falcon had torn. Green on one side, a layer of roots and dirt on the other, it looked like a carpet. He set the carpet of moss in the water green side down and it floated.

A raft! he thought. *You didn't kill me, falcon, you gave me a raft!* He quickly pulled up more moss and covered himself with it, wearing it like a hooded cape so the falcons wouldn't see him from the air. Then he gathered two long twigs and hurried out onto his raft, paddling with all the might and speed a mouse could muster.

♣ ♥ 19 ♦ ♠

Henry and Bernard

When he reached the far bank of the pond, Bernard jumped from his little ship. He laughed in triumph as he reached the winding footpath. His fur was muddy and the muscles in his arms were tired, but he had never felt so alive.

Partway down the path stood a line of business mice, waiting with suitcases in hand.

"What are you waiting for?" asked Bernard.

One of the business mice looked up.

"We're headed downtown," she said. Then she pointed to the first mouse in line.

Bernard watched as the mouse grabbed ahold of the edge of a man's trousers and pulled herself up. The man walked off in great strides and soon headed down the steps of the subway.

"Fastest way to get there," said the mouse.

The next several mice in line also pulled themselves up on the men and women walking by.

"How can you tell where they're going?" Bernard asked the business mouse.

"We work in the same offices," she said. "Where are you headed?"

"Chelsea," said Bernard.

"Ah," said the mouse. "You're in the wrong line."

She pointed to another group of mice, who looked very fit. Many of them were dressed in well-tailored black clothes. Some wore jewelry or sported beautiful drawings on their arms, and some had paintbrushes sticking out of their back pockets or thick-framed glasses. As he got closer, he noticed the mouse with the short whiskers from the flower market was waiting there in line—the mouse who had put the wreath of flowers around his neck.

"Hello!" Bernard said, happy to see a familiar face.

The mouse, whose name was Henry, turned to Bernard and smiled, then he hugged him.

"Bernard! Everyone has been talking about you. Did you bring help to stop the Pork Pie Gang?"

Bernard's moment of happiness disappeared like a soap bubble popping. He felt shabby and muddy and like he had let down his friends. He said, "I didn't, Henry. I found no help at all, and was very nearly trapped and killed myself. I'm sorry."

Henry squeezed Bernard's paw. "It's not your *fault*," he said kindly. "Shall we get a lift to the diner together?"

"You're headed there too?" Bernard asked.

"I don't know anyone who isn't!" said Henry. "Ivy has been telling every animal in town about the meeting."

Just then a tall man wearing a black tracksuit jogged by. Bernard and Henry grabbed the bottom cuff of his pants and swung themselves up.

The man ran out of the park and onto the sidewalk of the busy city, then down into the subway. Once they were on the platform, the mice let go of the man's pants and waited together in the crowded station. The train rushed in on a torrent of cold air and the mice hopped inside, scurrying beneath the seats to avoid being trampled by commuters.

"Look," Henry said, pointing to the wall of the train car.

Bernard's blood went cold. At the top of the wall, all along the car, were photographs of Gary's grinning face. They were advertisements for the ukulele concert—the same as the poster Leon had showed them in the underground.

PPGP Presents
The First, Last, and Only Endless Ukulele Concert!
Seven o'clock on May 25 at Times Square
All are welcome.
Free pickles.

There were only hours left until Pork Pie Gang's concert.

♣ ♥ 20 ♦ ♠

Cat and Queen

The train stopped at Twenty-Third Street. Bernard and Henry zigzagged through the crowd and up the steps, bursting out into the sunlight. They caught the pant leg of another commuter and rode it five blocks, jumping off right in front of the Empire Diner.

Bernard had imagined the place would look like a castle. It was, after all, where the queen held court, but it was nothing of the kind. It looked in fact like a train car—it was silver and sleek and had windows all along the side. The sign out front was in the shape of a beautiful skyscraper with a long antenna on top. The mice hurried to the back door of the diner.

"Shh," Henry said as they approached. "This place has a dangerous bouncer."

They peered around the corner and Bernard saw the back of a large black-and-white cat, its tail twitching. Part of its ear was missing, as if it had been cut with a scissor. There was a small pile of bone toothpicks at its feet.

"Mittens!" Bernard shouted. And Henry gave out a little shriek as the cat turned around.

"Bernard!" said Mittens, bounding over to him. "Look at you, you been rolling in the mud?" Mittens brushed Bernard's fur roughly, then gave him some pats on the back.

"I nearly gave up hope! I've been waiting for you for DAYS! Thought you were a goner."

Henry watched all of this in astonishment.

"You know Mittens the mouse hunter?" he asked.

"Hey!" said Mittens. "I ain't hunting no mice—I ain't the kind. I just make sure nobody's sneaking into the storeroom, that's all. Give 'em a scare; it's part of the job. But I ain't eating no mice. I don't know how those rumors got started."

"Because it's your job to terrorize mice!" said Henry indignantly.

"Whaddaya want?" said Mittens, grinning. "New York's a tough town, a cat's gotta hustle."

"It's okay," Bernard said. "Mittens is my friend."

"Dat's right!" said Mittens. "And I'm *your* friend too, you cute little pipsqueak. Any friend of Bernard's is a friend of mine. We ain't got time for fighting with each other—c'mon."

But Henry had no intention of going with Mittens, even if he was a friend of Bernard's. Instead he slipped through the back door and down the basement steps alone.

"His loss," said Mittens.

Mittens led Bernard through the back door of the diner into a crowded kitchen that smelled like coffee and every manner of delicious food. Cooks in white shirts were hard at work preparing lunch for customers. They were either too busy to notice or didn't mind at all that the animals were passing through.

A swinging door led out into the bright dining room where people sat eating, sunlight pouring in through the windows. Everything was silver and mirrored and lovely. She must be a very powerful queen, Bernard thought with relief. She would surely call on her guards to take care of the Pork Pie Gang; she might even know some magic.

Just then Bernard caught sight of her.

There in a corner was a tall older woman. She sat with perfect posture, wearing a red sequined gown, embroidered with white roses. Her eyes were dark and her lips were red and her hair was piled in shining black curls on top of her head. There were jewels around her neck, and she had a fierce, wise expression on her face. On the table before her was a teacup with pictures of hearts and clovers on it.

Her guards, a crow and four yellow finches, were perched on the window ledge outside, looking in at her. She was deep in conversation with two bees who were sitting in an orchid that stood in a tiny vase at the center of her table. And beneath her chair sat a little dog with a jeweled collar.

"Your Majesty," Mittens said. "This is Bernard Pepperlin."

Bernard bowed low and the queen looked down at him, raising an eyebrow. Then she lifted him up to the table, holding him gently in the palm of her hand. The crow and the finches fluttered their wings and stared at him.

"It's a pleasure to meet you," said Bernard.

She was elegant, but as Bernard got closer, he saw that she looked weary, as if she had been up all night.

"Bernard Pepperlin," she said. "So you are the little mouse who escaped the Pork Pie Gang and rallied the underground. You are the one who chased those weasels out of the flower market."

"I . . . ," Bernard stammered. "I didn't do it by myself."

"No, indeed," she said. "Nobody ever does."

He was wondering if she was going to tell them now how they could defeat the weasels, what sort of help she was going to give them.

"Since the beginning of my reign," said the queen, "weasels have been a problem. They're cruel and they're vicious and they're selfish and they're *unbearably* boring. I sometimes think being boring, being aggressively boring, is a kind of cruelty. Do you?"

"I . . . ," Bernard stammered again. "I don't think so."

"What *do* you think?" she asked.

"I think they don't know any better," he said.

"Ha!" said the queen, and her eyes glittered. "Don't know any better? Mouse, please. These weasels know exactly what they are doing. They're trying to bore us to death. Because they're bored to death. They're trying to make us all the same." She scratched Mittens on the head and gazed out the window, and Bernard realized that Mittens in some way belonged to her.

The queen took a sip of her tea. Sunlight streamed across the table and made the sequins in her dress glitter. Bernard watched the people eating, talking. He saw the waiters moving from table to table, pouring coffee and tea. He heard the clatter of dishes from the kitchen and the conversations of men and women nearby. How was it that the queen could understand the language of animals and insects when other people couldn't? And why was she all alone in this diner? Where was the rest of the royal family?

"How are we to fight them?" asked Bernard. Now, he thought, she would give him the power that she had. She would give him a magic weapon, or tell him she had already taken care of it. But she sat silently, looking out the window.

When she finally spoke, her voice was only a whisper.

"We fight the way we always do," said the queen. "With our voices and our bodies, until there's nothing left."

♣ ♥ **21** ♦ ♠

Ivy's Plan

That was it, Bernard thought. The queen couldn't help them. He had asked everyone in the underground to meet him at the Empire Diner. He had told them the queen could help—but the queen had no better idea how to fight the Pork Pie Gang than anyone else. All she could offer was understanding, but understanding wasn't enough anymore.

And how could you fight for your own freedom, he thought, if you were loyal to a queen?

He had told his friends that Allie could help them, but Allie didn't even understand the magic that was in her own room. All she wanted was a pet.

How could he have gotten so many things wrong?

After the queen dismissed him, Mittens led Bernard back through the swinging doors, then down a flight of stairs that led to a basement storeroom. They walked past rows of shelves and boxes, and Bernard could see why a mouse would want to live down there. It was warm and dry, and there were sacks of things that mice always kept on hand, like sugar and grain and potatoes. There were jars of peanut butter and rows of fruit pies and big cans of chocolate syrup.

At the back of the storeroom there was a small green door. Mittens rapped on it three times and a rabbit wearing a black sweater and black boots opened it, letting them inside a large, brightly lit room. It was filled with creatures from the underground, and mice from the flower market. Many of them were dressed in black. Ivy and Sophie and Leon were standing at the front of the room. Pictures of each member of the Pork Pie Gang, a map, and several diagrams hung on the walls around them.

Ivy looked up when Bernard came in and a smile broke across her face. He had never seen her looking stronger and more determined.

"Here he is now!" Ivy said, and the animals cheered.

He shook his head and there was silence. The hopeful smiles on his friends' faces disappeared and were replaced by fear and worry, but Ivy's intelligent gold eyes shone into his.

"It doesn't matter," she said. "We have the best luck of all to have you back."

Bernard felt his chest tightening and tears welling in his eyes. He didn't want to let his friends down, but it was a great relief to be back among them.

"All right," Ivy went on. "Here's what we know. According to the sparrows who landed here this afternoon, weasels have been gathering in different parts of the city since the sun came up. They're preparing to take over each neighborhood. At seven o'clock today the Pork Pie Gang will have a captive audience." She pointed at an area on the map as she spoke. "Maybe the biggest captive audience in history. And if that audience watches them—if they stand there and pay attention to their terrible songs—the city as we know it will be gone."

Several of the animals began to mutter among themselves.

"Tell us something we don't know!" cried an angry Chihuahua. "We've been hearing about some plan to fight these weasels for days. But I'm looking around and I say we got nothin'. All we got is a bunch of runaway pets and the same old rats from the underground telling us we can be free."

"Hey!" said Mittens. "Let the lizard talk!"

"Thank you, Mittens," Ivy said. She cleared her

throat and went on. "It's true. We don't have much. We're small. We're weaker than the weasels and Time is not on our side. It's true we might not win."

A hush fell over the crowd.

"And that's why I've made a meticulous six-point plan. The details are all here." Ivy took a pile of maps and instructions off the table and began handing them out to all the animals. "Everyone has a job to do, and it should go like this.

"Rabbits," she said, "you're our ears. We need you stationed at every corner of the square—

"Pigeons, starlings, sparrows, you'll be bringing messages from the rabbits and fighting from the air when necessary.

"Mice and rats and squirrels. Show yourselves! Your job is to scare people off the streets so they can't hear the song.

"Dogs, you're our voice. Howling helped break up the gang back at PPGP—and it just might work again.

"Bees, your help in the flower market did not go unnoticed and we remember the brave souls among you who fought the weasels there. I can't ask you to use your stingers—I know that it could kill you. But you too can scare creatures off the street, and like the dogs, you can raise your voices.

"Frogs and cats—by nature you are aloof. We just ask you to fight in any way you can.

"If you are hurt, head for the sewer grate. Rats will be waiting there to give medical attention and the crosstown ferry will be running all night, taking the injured back to the underground, where they can be safe."

By the time Ivy was done speaking, the animals had tears in their eyes. The task ahead of them seemed impossible. But they understood the code of all small animals, and if they died upholding that code, they would not die alone.

♣ ♥ **22** ♦ ♠

A Battle beneath the Bright Lights

An hour before the concert was to begin, the creatures began arriving at Times Square. Some came by the crosstown ferry, some by train or tunnel or sky.

When Bernard arrived, he could not believe his eyes. The place was so crowded with people it was nearly impossible to move without getting trampled. Lights flashed and images danced over the sides of the massive buildings that rose up around Times Square. The place crackled with electricity and color. Bright red and yellow and blue and green and orange lights and pictures filled every inch of their sight. It was as if someone had broken open the sky and filled it with advertisements. Advertisements for shows, for clothing, for people.

The streets were lined with restaurants and theaters. In some parts there were no cars, just more people walking, eating, gawking. Pigeons and small birds scavenged the sidewalks and streets. There were performers singing, dancing, and acting—working for tips from people passing by. And there was some kind of magic that could put the images of people standing in the square up on the buildings for everyone to see.

Bernard felt dizzy. For a moment he was hopeful the Pork Pie Gang would be lost in the crowd or ignored among the enchanted buildings and creatures. But then he saw them. They had set up a stage in the center of the square. Gary and the rest of the band stood together—and around them there were dozens of other weasels—standing guard, ready to protect them. People and animals had already begun to notice the gang, and they gathered around, waiting to see the ukulele concert.

Ivy raced up to Bernard's side.

"It's a matter of minutes now," she said. "The rabbits have given the word."

Bernard's heart thumped in his chest. Suddenly he heard squeals from the crowd.

"Ugh!" somebody cried. "It's a *rat*!"

"Oh no! There's another one!"

Bernard scurried up the back of a man's leg, onto his shoulder, and then onto his head. The man screamed. "There's mice everywhere!" The man swiped wildly at Bernard, but Bernard managed to jump away, landing on another person in the crowd.

Soon voices rose from all parts of the square. "Help!" "That's disgusting!" "A rat just took my potato chips!"

"There's a lizard in my shopping bag!" "A squirrel stole my coffee!"

The small animals were suddenly everywhere—running wild. Birds swooping, bees swarming; Johnny the Squirrel raced from person to person, untying their shoes. A group of tough-looking mice wearing red jackets with the letters *MM* painted on the back scurried along, taunting people as they left shops and theaters. Sophie, two bedraggled racoons, and an angry yipping Chihuahua chased tourists down into the subway.

But there were not enough of them to prevent the Pork Pie Gang from starting their terrible song.

Toc. Toc. Toc. Toc. Gary began tapping his pen against his horrible straight teeth. Three other weasels began plucking their ukuleles and the singer with the screeching, yowling voice began to sing. The grating noise joined the sounds of car horns beeping and alarms sounding.

♠

Zooba zooba zooba zooba zooba zooba zay
Today it won't matter what you say
I drove a car I bought a house
I flew a plane
I ate a mouse
I wore a fancy feathered hat
I taxidermied your favorite cat
And pulled the whiskers off a rat

The song's power was beginning to take hold. People stood fascinated by the droning, screeching ugliness of it all. It seemed to Bernard that many of the people enjoyed the terrible song. They were taking pictures, giving the gang even more attention. It was already difficult to say how long the weasels had been playing.

Bernard looked out at the crowd and could see even more people gathering. He tried his best to frighten them off, but the air felt thick and heavy, and he found himself growing tired. To his left several rats from the underground were limping along, trying to get closer to the band. One of them looked like his leg had been broken. He stumbled with his arms draped across the shoulders of his friends.

"Get him to the sewer grate!" Bernard shouted.

Bernard spotted Leon, whose face was swollen and bleeding. He watched as Leon climbed up a streetlamp and then jumped onto the shoulder of man who was pointing a camera at the Pork Pie Gang's concert. The man screamed and Leon knocked the camera to the ground, where it was trampled by the crowd.

Bernard looked around for Ivy, but he couldn't see her anywhere. Above their heads a dark cloud of insects was buzzing and swarming. He could feel the song doing its terrible work. The images on the buildings that had been flickering and moving were now standing still. Cars had come to a halt. Business mice looked at their watches, tapping them as if they were broken. Even in the midst of the fight, in the midst of such a crowd, a great feeling of emptiness and timelessness was descending upon them.

Then suddenly he spotted it. About half a block from where the weasels had set up their stage was a chalk circle, and all around it a small crowd was slowly beginning to gather.

"Over here," Bernard shouted. "Over here, everyone—this is the *real* show—a real showstopper!" He zipped through the crowd toward the cockroaches, calling to every manner of creature to join them.

At the center of the circle, the cockroaches were setting up their band.

"Boy oh boy oh boy!" shouted the bandleader. "Good thing we brought earplugs today, ladies and gentlemen, rats and mice, pigeons and starlings, bees and frogs. Would you get a load of that lousy song? Who do those weasels think they are?"

Skippy Waterburg, the Girl from the Silverware Drawer herself, stood next to him shaking her head, her antennae waving from side to side. "I'd say *we* could do better than that!" she said. "Whaddaya think?"

The little crowd that had gathered around them clapped and whooped. "Sing it, Skippy!"

The cockroach band started playing. And it seemed to Bernard that there were many more members than he'd seen before. Strings and trombones and clarinets and drums, and then the wonderful tap-tap-tapping of the dancers.

"The city is *ours!*" Skippy shouted.

And then she began to sing:

The city is ours, it's ours!
Every crevice and every crack
Every train and every track
Every Tompkins Square squirrel, or small boat that sails
All the art on walls, all the yellow leaves in fall
The city is ours, it's ours

Suddenly a bigger crowd had gathered around the cockroaches. People leaving Broadway shows stopped to watch them perform. People who had been watching the weasels came to watch Skippy singing and dancing and twirling and flying. Soon people were taking pictures of the cockroaches.

"We're not loud enough," Skippy shouted. "We're gonna need your help!"

All the cockroaches were singing, but soon the rats and mice and runaway pets joined in. Even the bees hummed along, and Glub hopped forward into the chalk circle beside Skippy and added his melodic baritone to the mix. It was a familiar song—one the troupe had performed all over the city. The melody was so catchy no one could forget it. They sang:

Wading in fountains or skating on ice
Singing on street corners dancing with mice

Walking at midnight to see the bright lights

The city is ours, it's ours

Basements and rooftops and high water towers

Sidewalks and streetlamps and bouquets of flowers

Hot summer pavement and cool thunder showers

The city is ours, it's ours

The food has magical powers

Pho and masala, a slice for a dollah

dim sum and sushi, a pineapple smoothie

The city is ours, it's ours!

The bridges and trains, the sun and the rains

The birds and the beasts, the hunger, the feasts

The queens and the kings, the dawning of spring

The barges and parks and each dog who barks

All of it sings like a song in our hearts

The city is ours, it's ours

Bernard could feel it—things were speeding up
again; the voices of every kind of creature had drowned

out the slovenly screeching and tapping of the Pork Pie Gang.

The crowd was cheering "Brava!" and "Go, Skippy!" and "We did it!"

In the commotion no one seemed to notice that Gary had left the stage and was pushing his way through the crowd, baring his teeth and snarling. Skippy raised four of her arms and was taking a bow and blowing kisses. She never saw what was coming.

Before anyone could stop him, Gary leapt into the middle of the chalk circle and, with a great stomp, crushed Skippy beneath his foot.

♣ ♥ **23** ♦ ♠

From the Air

The crowd gasped. They rushed at Gary but he pulled out his knife. Soon his guards were surrounding him and moving in on the small animals, taking out twine to bind their paws.

Bernard kicked against a weasel, dodging the blade of its knife. But Ivy, who was fighting beside him, wasn't so lucky. The weasel lunged at her, slicing with the blade, cutting her tail clean off. She cried out in anger and pain. Bernard grabbed her hand and pulled her toward the entrance of the sewer grate.

"We need help!" he cried.

"No, let go," she said, struggling against him. "It'll grow back; we've got to keep going."

The crowd around the chalk circle stood weeping, hugging one another. Some rats had gathered around Skippy, ready to help. But the cockroaches shrugged and shook their heads and kept playing their song. The bandleader continued to talk to Skippy as if she wasn't crushed against the pavement.

"This is too awful to watch," said Ivy. "Why aren't they trying to help her?"

Just then Skippy's antennae rose up.

"It must be a reflex," said one of the rats. "Someone should really cover her with a sheet."

Then Skippy's wings opened and closed. Soon the small animals were watching in awe as Skippy propped herself up on two of her elbows and shook her head roughly from side to side. The other cockroaches began clapping in time with the music—and though she was still partly stuck to the sidewalk, Skippy gave a big grin.

"Wow," she said. "What a sore loser!"

"Yeah, what a jerk that guy was," said the bandleader. "How you feeling, Skippy?"

"Oh fine, fine," she said. She sat up on her knees, gave herself another shake, then stood on two feet. "Ready, boys? Show must go on!"

Just as she began to dance, a sparrow touched down in front of Bernard.

"Mr. Pepperlin," said the sparrow. "The rabbits say they've heard plans about another attack. They say they can feel it."

"What do you mean?"

"From the sky," said the sparrow. She looked up and

pointed her wing toward the tops of the buildings. "The rabbits say we're in danger. They've already taken shelter in the subway."

Bernard looked up at the tall buildings. In this part of town, it wasn't a forest of buildings like down in the East Village. Here the buildings were like mountains. He squinted up at the massive skyrises and then caught sight of her—perched on a roof, her feathers glowing in the flicker of lights.

It was Hunter. She was quietly watching the commotion on the ground, getting ready to strike. Bernard turned and saw more falcons; the tops of nearly every building had at least one standing guard, stoic and determined. It would be difficult for them to strike in the middle of such a large crowd, but Bernard knew how determined these birds were.

"Quick," said Bernard. "We've got to take cover. Let everyone know—head for the stage."

"The stage?" cried Ivy. "You're crazy! You mean the subway? We have to get underground!"

"No!" said Bernard. "Everyone take shelter under the weasels' stage. Now!"

As he said it, a flash of gray and white raced across their vision. A falcon, diving from the top of a brightly lit tower, swooped down and nearly grabbed the mouse in the hula skirt and sparkly red shoes. He shrieked and threw himself on the ground.

Now all the small animals began to run in a panic. "Head for the stage!" Bernard called out. "Head for the stage!" cried the pigeons and sparrows and starlings. Soon the small animals were running for their lives, leading the falcons to the weasels.

They dove beneath the stage and the falcons swooped down, just missing them but not missing the weasels. They grasped the weasels in their sharp talons. The weasels lunged at the birds with their knives, but they were no match, and one by one the Pork Pie Gang was plucked up into the sky or felled with a single peck. Never had birds of prey helped small creatures as they did that day.

Finally, only Gary remained. Standing on the stage, shrieking and cursing and waving his knife.

Bernard watched as a beautiful bird with dark, yellow-rimmed eyes circled above the stage. It was Hunter. She looked majestic and free, gliding on currents of air between the tops of the buildings.

Then she turned and swooped down. Faster than fast her sharp talons aimed right for Gary. At the moment she struck, she closed her eyes—then opened them again and looked right at Bernard, giving him a nod.

She let out a cry of triumph as she flew up and up and up, heading east toward the river, the weasel still cursing and flailing in her talons, until she was out of sight.

The small creatures of the underground crept out from beneath the stage. The city was filled with sound and color and light; cars were speeding past and people gazed at the sky in astonishment. All that was left of the Pork Pie Gang was the flutter of feathered hats falling and scattering like litter on the streets of Times Square.

♣ ♥ **24** ♦ ♠

Bernard of the Flowers

Bernard raised the gate on the shop at West Twenty-Eighth Street and brought the bundles of violets inside, separating them into bouquets.

It had been two weeks since the battle at Times Square.

After the creatures made their way back to the underground, after they cared for the injured, after they had a party with chocolate cake and Skippy singing a ballad to commemorate the day, Bernard had many decisions to make.

The queen knighted him and offered him a job in her court, along with the crow and the yellow finches and Mittens.

Mittens asked Bernard to come live with him and offered him a job fishing on the river.

Leon and Ivy asked him to join the underground and dedicate his life to freeing small animals from their troubles.

But Henry knew what Bernard really wanted, and asked him if he would like to run the shop next door to his own. Now each day Bernard woke with the sun and unloaded bundles and bales and bouquets of flowers. He talked with customers and made them tea. The shop was cozy and smelled like the garden. Inside, there was a long table and chairs for all his friends.

Each day Mittens came by to chat on his way to sit with the queen. He always brought Bernard a dragon fruit.

And Ivy came by too, dressed in her black sweater and cap, to deliver the underground newspaper.

Glub stopped in for tea and always bought crocuses to take home.

The mouse with the hula skirt and sparkly red shoes, and the sparrows and starlings and bees, came by to gossip. But the cockroaches rarely came to the flower district. They were too busy rehearsing because *The Girl from the Silverware Drawer* had at long last become a Broadway show.

Bernard wrapped up a bouquet of violets and snowdrops and baby's breath and tied it with a red ribbon, handing it to Ivy.

"You sure it's no trouble?" he asked.

"No trouble at all," Ivy said. "Skippy's going to love them."

"Tell them all congratulations for me," Bernard said. "Tell them Henry and I will catch the show next week."

"Will do," said Ivy. She put the flowers in the basket

of her bicycle, then turned and smiled before getting on and heading north.

"The city is ours, Bernard!" she called as she pedaled up Eighth Avenue.

He laughed and stuck a flower behind his ear. "It's ours, Ivy! It's ours!"

♣ ♥ ♦ ♠

ACKNOWLEDGMENTS

I would like to thank my editor, Claudia Gabel, for making this book possible; Jin Auh, for her guidance and sound advice; and my agent, Anna Stein, for helping me navigate the new world of writing for children. A fellowship from the MacDowell Foundation provided the quiet and community necessary to work on multiple projects, including *Bernard Pepperlin*. Early conversations with Zane Lepson about bugs, pigeons, cats, and cabdrivers provided great insight. Selena

Samuella brainstormed to find Bernard Pepperlin his name. She is a star. My dedicated first reader, Jamie Newman, listened to multiple drafts and helped Ivy to envision her six-point plan. Jennifer Chen's last-minute artistry was a lifesaver. My father, John Shannon, read an early draft of this novel and gave me wonderful notes, including a brief history of the pork pie hat. His limitless promotion of my work makes me think HarperCollins should put him on the payroll. Thanks, Dad! My mother, Kaye Newbury, read to me every day of my childhood, many days of my adolescence, and just the other day over the phone. Thanks, Mom! Thanks to my new friend Jude Henry Kahn and to his parents for their love and encouragement. The final scenes of this book were written sitting on their big blue couch. Thanks to Dove and Herman and Kai and to Dr. Mina Lepson for jokes and inspiring conversations. I'm grateful that I share a life and a loft with Marc Lepson. Go, Sweater Team! The City Is Ours, ML! Thanks to my coach, Pete Shapiro, and to my tai chi buddies at the Chinatown Y. Thanks to my uncle Franklin Crawford, a giant among men. Thanks to Eli and Em, who read early drafts and wrote amazing songs and taught me about happiness and the inner lives of mice. Go, Mouse Family. Thanks to Asa Horvitz, Corinne Manning, Ben Durham, Emma Heaney, and T Clutch Fleischman, for inspiring conversations, book recommendations, and frog catching. When writing a character like Ivy it's good to have some real-world inspiration—so I'm lucky to have grown up beside Ann Godwin, who helped me build a house in the top of a lilac tree, braved bike wrecks and woodland adventures, always knew when the ice was too thin, got the best grades, did the most pull-ups, and once helped me carry a giant plywood ice-cream cone for a mile, through every backyard in town; suffice it to say, characters like lock-picking revolutionaries who can run upside down and explain the nature of time don't just pop into one's head from thin air. Thanks, Ann!

Read on for a sneak peek at
Cara Hoffman's next heartwarming fable,
The Ballad of Tubs Marshfield

Tubs was the brightest, the greenest; a frog among frogs ready to burst into song. He sported a gold-and-crimson vest and smiled like he had just heard a joke. Tubs could be counted on. His eyes were the color of the sun setting over the water, and he could swim from day to night and back again.

Tubs made his home in the roots of an old mangrove tree. Cattails grew wild in the shallow water by the porch where his boat was moored. On windy days he would watch them dancing, their long slender bodies bowing over the marsh, all of them humming the same tune. Spider lily and trumpet vines climbed the walls of his house, the scent of their flowers drifting through the swamp like a distant melody.

The swamp was so serene, few ever ventured into the wider world. Even the birds, who could fly great distances, stayed put. Everything they needed was right there.

The roof of Tubs's house was open to let in the wind, sun, and stars. Inside, the walls were lined with jars of dried bluebottle flies and bright red rosemallow wine, which he served on special occasions. Tubs's trombone, washboard, jaw harp, and clarinet lay out in the living room, ready to use. His piano—which was missing quite a few keys—grinned out from beneath a pile of papers, pots and pans, and fishing poles. Above his kitchen sink, Tubs had hung a portrait of his aunt Elodie, rest her soul, who had traveled as far as New Orleans and was known for having the most beautiful voice in all the swamp.

Life was a song for Tubs. During the day he hopped

among the reeds and saw grass, or put on high rubber boots and went fishing, sitting on the bank with
the dragonflies and snapping turtles. Sometimes he
cooled in the dark water, sheltered by tall cypresses
and the lush leaves of the mangrove trees. At midday,
you could find him drifting, just beneath the surface of
the swamp, his gold eyes gazing toward the hot blue
heaven of the Louisiana sky.

But nothing compared to life when the sun went
down and the music of the night rose up all around.
The song of the water and the stones, the song of the
cicadas and the leaves, the song of the ground and the
paws, the howl of the fox and the wind. The near silence
of the moths and the rabbits; a symphony of rustling
and pauses of fluttering and digging. The birds singing
their warbled questions to the night, the fish's bright
splash like a faint cymbal crash. And down in the hol-
lows of the mangroves—in the houses of the frogs—a
night of reeling and song that would last until dawn.

Frogs in their boats, frogs on their porches, frogs in the mud, and in the branches of trees—and Tubs at the center of it all—his house open to the world.

Tubs loved the swamp at night. Especially the summer he still had a tail and Aunt Elodie would wear her crown of lightning bugs and the mud and reeds smelled wonderful and little fires blazed over the water in the distance.

Elodie had a daughter named Lila, who was Tubs's favorite cousin—and the two did everything together. When they were small, they would jump off the dock, pretending they could fly. They swam in the cool water and trekked through the forest of cattails. They fished near the garden of lily pads and talked to the water rats and ducks. While Tubs made up songs and dances and learned how to play just about any instrument, Lila read books. She liked to tell people things they didn't know and fix things that were broken.

In the evening they would talk to the swallows who

came out to play as the last rays of sun shimmered over the surface of the swamp. At night they would lie in the red-and-white boat together looking up at the stars, eating mayflies and falling asleep to the high sweet sound and to the low bass drawl of their aunts and uncles, cousins and great-uncles, parents, step-parents, and godparents, nieces and nephews, brothers and sisters. Dozens of generations of frogs all living in the same place, spotted and speckled, green and yellow and mottled brown, large and small.

"Just look at that moon!" said Tubs one evening in early June. "How can anyone keep quiet when it's shining so silver?"

"The song they're singing now," Lila told him, "is two hundred and sixty-five MILLION years old." She poked him and he grinned. "Did you hear me? It's the first song our ancestors made up."

Tubs listened for a minute. Two hundred and sixty-five million years was a long time to be singing the same song. It made him want to go get his clarinet and make up something new.

"You can't make up something new," Lila said. "Every bit of water on earth is the same water that was here to begin with. And we're all made of the creatures who came before us, and microscopic beings inhabit every inch of us."

"Huh?" said Tubs.

Lila said, "It's hard to improve on 'Kiss Me, I'm the Fattest.' If there was a better song, someone would have written it by now. Anyway," Lila said, "look at this." She pulled a letter from her pocket and handed it to Tubs. "I haven't shown anyone yet." It was postmarked with a fancy blue-and-yellow seal—an image of a hand reaching out of the sky, holding a book.

Tubs unfolded the letter and read. It made his skin feel dry. It was from a place called the Sorbonne, which as far as he could tell was not in Louisiana. He looked up at Lila. "Where is this place?"

"In Paris," she said. "It's a school."

"Where's Paris?"

"It's across a big salt pond."

At first Tubs thought he might cry—thinking about Lila leaving was awful. But then he looked at the letter again and his heart soared for his cousin's good news. "Lila!" Tubs shouted, jumping to his feet. "Lila! This is amazing! Elodie," he called from the boat, waving the letter above his head. "Elodie, break out the rose-mallow wine; break out the bluebottles! Lila is going to school! Everyone, everyone, Lila is going to school!"

Tubs remembered Lila's face that night, how happy she was, and how proud Aunt Elodie was. And how long the party lasted. And how they changed the words of that old song to "kiss me, I'm the smartest." And how Lila explained to them that it didn't technically make it a new song if you changed one word. And how he ate too many bluebottles. And how the turtles came over to offer their congratulations and an owl flew down and stood on the bank of the marshy expanse and talked seriously to Lila. And how the bullfrogs puffed out their necks when she walked by. But the thing he remembered the most was how she smiled. He had never seen Lila smile the way she had that night—when she was about to leave the place he loved the most.